About the Author

Laurie Faria Stolarz was raised in Salem, Massachusetts, and educated at Merrimack College in North Andover. She has an MFA in creative writing and a graduate certificate in screenwriting, both from Emerson College in Boston. She currently teaches writing and French. Her other books include *Blue Is for Nightmares, White Is for Magic, and Red Is for Remembrance.*

Visit her website at www.lauriestolarz.com.

To Write to the Author

If you wish to contact the author or would like more information about this book, please write to the author in care of Llewellyn Worldwide and we will forward your request. Both the author and publisher appreciate hearing from you and learning of your enjoyment of this book and how it has helped you. Llewellyn Worldwide cannot guarantee that every letter written to the author can be answered, but all will be forwarded. Please write to:

Laurie Faria Stolarz
℅ Llewellyn Worldwide
2143 Wooddale Drive, Dept. 978-0-7387-0631-3
Woodbury, MN 55125-2989, U.S.A.

Please enclose a self-addressed stamped envelope for reply,
or $1.00 to cover costs. If outside U.S.A., enclose
international postal reply coupon.

Many of Llewellyn's authors have websites with additional information and resources. For more information, please visit our website at:

www.llewellyn.com

Silver is for Secrets

Laurie Faria Stolarz

Llewellyn Publications
Woodbury, Minnesota

FIRST EDITION
Eighth Printing, 2008

Editing by Megan C. Atwood, Andrew Karre and Rebecca Zins
Cover design by Gavin Dayton Duffy
Cover image © ImageClick/TIPS Images

Llewellyn is a registered trademark of Llewellyn Worldwide, Ltd.

Library of Congress Cataloging-in-Publication Data
Stolarz, Laurie Faria, 1972–
    Silver is for secrets / Laurie Faria Stolarz.—1st ed.
        p. cm.
    Summary: During a summer vacation at the beach with friends, eighteen-year-old hereditary witch Stacey has more nightmares which involve Clara, a new girl with a talent for causing trouble.
    ISBN 13: 978-0-7387-0631-3
    ISBN 10: 0-7387-0631-0
    [1. Witchcraft—Fiction. 2. Magic—Fiction. 3. Dreams—Fiction. 4. Extrasensory perception—Fiction. 5. Revenge—Fiction.] I. Title.

PZ7.S8757Si 2005
[Fic]—dc22

2004057816

Llewellyn Publications
A Division of Llewellyn Worldwide, Ltd.
2143 Wooddale Drive, Dept. 978-0-7387-0631-3
Woodbury, MN 55125-2989, U.S.A.
www.llewellyn.com

Printed in the United States of America

For Ed, Mom, and Ryan,
with love and gratitude

Acknowledgments

How do you thank the person who's been there since the first word of *Blue;* who's read all your drafts, every single one; who turns your pages around, often within a twenty-four-hour period, regardless of how busy she is? The person who supports you and cheers you on; who's often more excited about your work than you are, even twenty drafts later? Lara Zeises, I really don't know how to thank you. You're an invaluable friend and critique partner, and one of the most talented writers I know.

Special thanks to my fabulous Llewellyn editors, Megan Atwood, Andrew Karre, and Becky Zins. Your attention to detail, continuous encouragement, invaluable suggestions, and sense of humor make the writing and editing process all the more enjoyable.

Thanks to Lee Ann Faria for reading one of the final drafts of *Silver*—I appreciate your careful attention to detail. Thanks to Tea Benduhn and Steven Goldman, who have been there since *Blue*, and read pieces of *Silver*. Thanks also to Lieutenant Fran Hart of the Burlington, Massachusetts, Police Department for answering my questions regarding nautical law.

Finally, many, many thanks to all the friends and family members in my corner—you know who you are—and to all the fans I've met, who've e-mailed, and who've written me letters of support and encouragement; it's really the best part.

one

It's late, past 3 AM, but I can't fall asleep. I feel like there's this tugging inside me, like an invisible rope is attached to my gut and someone's pulling at it from the other end, urging me to stay awake.

I do my best to temper the feeling—I flip-flop a couple times in bed, rub patchouli and peppermint oils at the pulse points on my neck, and even haul my butt out of bed to make a dream sachet out of dried lavender and rosemary—

normally surefire fixes for temporary insomnia. But it's just no use. The more I try to ignore it, the tighter the knot in my gut becomes. I just can't shake it—the gnawing, incessant feeling that something horrible is about to happen.

I crawl out of bed, once again, and step into a pair of fuzzy slippers, doing my best to keep quiet so I don't wake Drea and Amber, asleep in their beds only a few feet away. I throw a sweatshirt on over my cotton PJs, grab a few spell supplies, and head out to the beach behind our cottage.

The moon is in full view, smack dab in the middle of a blue-black sky, the two dark colors swirling together like a giant slab of marble. I find myself a spot just in front of the water where the outgoing tide meets the sand and sit back on my heels. The warm, salty breeze sweeps over my face and combs at my hair tangles, sending spicy tingles all over my skin.

I remove the necessary spell supplies from my bag—a jar of sea salt and a Thermos full of moon-bathed rainwater. My grandmother, who taught me most of what I know about spells, used to stress the importance of offering up gifts to nature. She used to say that what we offer up to the universe comes back to us threefold.

I sink down into the cool, powdery sand and stare up at the moon's fullness, imagining the light soaking into my skin, the energy awakening my soul. I pour the sea salt into the Thermos and hold it up to the moon's light. Then I say, "O fullest moon, on this night of dread, please accept this gift from the ocean's bed. And I ask thee, with a heart so pure, to help my body tell me more. Blessed be the way."

I dig a six-inch hole in the sand and pour the mixture inside, patting a layer of rocks over the top as a cover. Then I lie back and stare up at the moon, thinking how much I've changed these past couple years, how it wasn't so long ago that I used my spells to try and stop what my body and senses were trying to warn me. Now I'm using my spells to summon forth these same instincts. I close my eyes and concentrate on my body and what it can tell me, imagining the moon's energy drawing forth the answers from deep within my core.

But I don't feel anything. After several minutes spent meditating on the spell, I have no better idea of why I can't sleep than I did before coming out here. So what is it? What's this feeling inside me? Why can't I relax? Why do I feel like the seams of my world are about to rip wide open?

But unfortunately the answers don't come that easily. I know I need to get some sleep. I grab my Thermos and head back to my room, leaving the moon's gift on the beach.

I lie back against the coolness of my sheets, suddenly feeling a bit more centered, more relaxed. I imagine the moon's energy penetrating through the ceiling and my bed covers, casting right over me, easing me to sleep.

The next thing I know, I'm covered in it.

I wake up a couple hours later and find it everywhere—on my pillow, the bed sheet, matted to the tips of my hair. I sit up in bed and notice dark cherry-red stains on my forearms and wrists. A knot forms inside my chest. I do my best to unbind it, to inhale a calming breath.

"Stacey?" Drea asks, rolling over in bed. "Are you okay?"

But I can't answer. I go to wipe my face, noticing more stains. My hand trembles over my lips, trying to hold it all in, but then a trickle of blood rolls over my fingers.

The light clicks on in our room. "Oh my god!" Drea rushes out of bed. "Stacey, what happened?"

I pinch my nose closed to try and make the bleeding stop and look around the room for a box of tissues.

Amber sits up in bed and leans over her Superman blow-up doll to get a better look.

Still holding my nose, I end up swiping a sock from the floor and pressing it to my nose. "I'm fine," I tell them through a wad of cotton. "I dust hat a little dosebeed."

"A *little* nosebleed?" Drea questions.

"You look like Carrie freakin' White at the prom," Amber says.

"*Who?*" Drea asks.

"Carrie White. You know? Stephen King's *Carrie.*"

I ignore their banter and press the sock into my nose to try and clot the bleeding, knowing that I should be grateful, that this is obviously the response I was praying for, that I did the spell for. I wanted my body to communicate to me, to give me insight—a clue, basically—into why I'm feeling so unhinged. And so this is it. I look down at the spattering of blood on my pillow, wondering what it could possibly mean.

"You're supposed to tilt your head back," Drea says.

"Not unless you want to drink it down," Amber corrects.

"So disgusting." Drea reaches into the mini-fridge for a pint of Ben & Jerry's. "Here," she says. "I think you're supposed to hold something cold at the back of your head to stop the bleeding."

I place the Chunky Monkey against my nose instead and glance at the clock; it's just after six—at least two hours of sleep, and yet I can't remember what I dreamt about.

I blot my nose to make sure the bleeding has stopped and move over to the dresser mirror to have a look for myself. It's even worse than I thought. It looks as though I've been beaten. There are patches of blood at the sides of my nose and over my lips. I grab a strand of my long, dark hair, the end now soiled with red. I wonder how long my nose was bleeding before I woke up, how I possibly could have slept through all this mess.

I sit down on the edge of my bed and silently count to ten. I wonder if I even dreamt anything at all. And, if I did, if it had anything to do with blood. I shake my head because I just don't know. Because the only thing that seems sure is that I can't break this feeling—this morguelike heaviness that sits on my heart and presses down into my gut.

"Um, Stace, no offense, but you're totally grossing me out here." Drea sweeps her hair up and secures it with an elastic; the loopy golden mass sits like a crown atop her head. "Don't you think you should clean yourself up?"

"Not to mention the crime scene you've got going on your pillow," Amber adds. She points to the bloody splotches on my bed.

I fish my bathrobe from the recyclable pile of laundry on the floor. "I'm gonna go take a shower."

"At least this'll teach you not to go digging for treasure." Amber clutches Superman extra tight, one of her numerous mini raspberry-red pigtails poking right into his eye.

I respond by closing the door behind me.

two

After a shower and a cleansing walk on the beach, I head back to the cottage. To my surprise, everyone is up. While PJ overnukes box after box of microwavable egg-and-cheese sandwiches in the kitchen, Amber butter-and-Nutellas the toast; Chad flips through the sports section of the *Cape Cod Gazette* in the adjoining living room; and Jacob watches TV.

Jacob pauses from channel surfing and comes to greet me with a kiss. "Hey, beautiful."

"Hey there," I say, pressing myself into his embrace, like a breath of fresh ocean air.

"Enough already," Amber says, dunking her finger into the Nutella jar and licking a giant fingerful. "If the cook's not getting any action for breakfast, then nobody else should either. It's a matter of respect."

"Say no more, butter biscuit." PJ says, licking his greasy finger. "I can cook for hours."

"I'm hardly in the mood for string beans."

I hear the blow dryer click on and off a couple times in the bedroom. Drea has this thing about blow-drying her hair upside down so that it goes all wild, and then she spends the next hour and a half putting each strand back in place, one by one.

Chad pauses from his newspaper to glance down at Jacob's grip on my hand, making me almost feel like I should pull away. But I don't. It's just so weird to be vacationing all together. I mean, it's one thing when you're in school, in classes, in the cafeteria, and pretending it isn't unbelievably awkward to see your ex with someone else. But it's a completely different thing when your ex is dating *his* ex and *that* ex just happens to be your best friend. Then, toss in the added awkwardness that comes with living together and, before you know it, your current significant other can feel completely ex-ed out. Translation: Chad and I are exes. Chad is dating Drea. I am dating Jacob. We're all vacationing under one roof.

Jacob is sensing our drama.

I squeeze Jacob's hand and lead him over to the table to set it up. Meanwhile, PJ has apparently aborted his microwave-egg-in-a-box idea, having pulled a carton of real eggs from the fridge. He's attempting to fry them in a spaghetti pot.

"So how's the snout?" Amber asks me. "Me and Drea were super scared for you. I mean, you looked like a freakin' chainsaw massacre."

PJ revs the blender a couple times for drama. "Amber told us all how you picked your nose to its bloody death."

I ignore him and look toward Jacob, sensing that he can tell something's wrong, something beyond just a normal nosebleed. He stares at me hard and bites the corner of his lip, almost as though he expects me to get right down to it. But I look away, trying to keep things light. For now at least.

"I'm fine," I say, plunking a couple plates down on the table.

"Well, that's a relief," Amber says. "Just let me know if I'll need to do anything drastic, like wear a raincoat to bed tonight."

"You *could* move in with PJ," I say.

Amber turns to look at him, at the egg yolk he's got dripping from his chin. "I'll take your primitive habits over his disgusting ones any day."

"They're hardly habits," I say.

"Whatever," she says. "Me, you, and Drea, bunking in together, just like old times—it's really the only surefire way to keep everybody from killing each other."

She definitely has a point, which is why we did end up with the parent-friendly sleeping arrangements.

"Or maybe, my little temptress, it's just your way of safe-guarding yourself from taking advantage of me in the middle of the night." PJ snarls at Amber.

"Oh, please," Amber says. "If I had to room with you—"

"What?"

Amber grabs an egg from the carton and cracks it into the spaghetti pot-turned-frying pan. "Any questions?"

"So you're okay?" Chad asks. "I mean, you don't need to see a doctor? My dad had to get his nose cauterized."

"He must have quite the picker," PJ says, faking a dig by scratching the side of his nose.

"I'm fine," I say, clearing my throat.

"Yeah," PJ repeats. "She's fine. I mean, it's not like she started whizzing the bed again."

"Or puking her guts up," Amber says, as if we need the reminder.

"Or anything else juicy." PJ dips his fingers into the bowl of eggs he's beating, pulling forth a handful of the slimy white part. It oozes through his fingers and drops back into the bowl in one gooey plop.

Sometimes I absolutely despise my friends. They're talking about last year when I was puking non-stop—a side effect of the nightmares I was having. And the year before that when my nightmares were causing me to wet the bed.

Jacob continues to stare at me. I know he wants to talk about my nosebleed. I want to talk about it, too. Just not right now—not in front of everyone like this. I mean, this was supposed to be a fun vacation, a stress-free summer.

A walk on the normal side.

"So why is everybody up so early?" I ask, in an effort to change the subject.

"It wasn't by choice," Amber says. "After you left, PJ thought it would be funny to act like he was eleven years old again. So he snuck into our room to dunk my hand into a bowl of water."

"So Miss Priss here goes all Fright Night on me and wakes the whole house up with her cowardly cries. I mean, seriously," PJ says, smearing a knifeful of tartar sauce on his egg and cheese sandwich, "does she need to pay a little visit to the great and powerful Oz for a smidgen of courage?"

"No," Amber says, "but maybe *you* should pay him a visit for a smidgen of maturity."

"What's that supposed to mean?"

"If the pacifier fits." She stuffs a fingerful of Nutella into his mouth to shut him up.

"Don't go tempting me with your kinky ideas of seduction, my little vixen," he says, happily licking up the chocolate on his lips.

PJ puckers up to Amber, but she responds by messing up his hair, the short, gravity-defying spikes bleached a Ken-doll platinum color—to go with the whole beach vibe, I imagine.

"Did someone say vixen?" Drea enters the living room and takes a seat next to Chad. She drapes her legs over his lap and over the sports section. And suddenly I'm reminded of just why she spends so long doing her hair. I mean, it's perfect—shampoo-commercial perfect. Shiny, bouncy, golden waves with just the right amount of tousling.

I grab a strand of my own hair, noting that it feels a little drier than normal and that I could probably use a trim.

The doorbell rings and Amber jumps from the table, practically trampling over everything in her pathway to the door—me included. "Maybe it's one of the frat-boy yummies from next door. I thought I saw one of them scoping me out yesterday." She pulls at the wedge in her Superwoman swim shorts, finger-counts her pigtails—seven, her lucky number—and then whips the door open so hard that it crashes against the wall.

"Looks like someone's a little hard up," Drea says.

Amber ignores the comment, her patty cake smile falling *splat* to the ground.

There's a girl standing there, maybe a couple of years younger than us but undeniably cute. The kind of cute you see on one of the shows on MTV—long and straight henna-red hair, heart-shaped face with yellow-tinted sunglasses, super tight T-shirt with long bell sleeves, and one of those sarong things that looks like a skirt. I peek at Jacob to see if he's noticed, but he's completely zoned himself out, watching some talk show on TV, the audience barking in the background.

"Yeah?" Amber says.

"Hi. I'm Clara. I was just wondering if Marcy and Greg are staying at this—"

"Wait," Amber says, interrupting her. "Don't I know you from someplace?"

Clara cocks her head slightly, as though trying to place Amber as well. "Were you at the Clam Stripper yester—?"

"Forget it," Amber says. She takes a step forward to look past the girl, hoping, I think, that she's brought along some WB-looking male friends. "Are you staying next door?" She points to the cottage at the right, where the fraternity guys have hung up their banner, the giant Greek letters ΔΠ marking their frat-boy territory.

"Yeah," Clara chirps, pointing in the opposite direction. "I'm a few houses down."

"Uh-huh."

"So Marcy and Greg *aren't* staying here?" Clara peeps at us over Amber's shoulder.

"Who?" Amber looks thoroughly annoyed now. She makes a big sigh and looks downward to assess the chippage to her pedicure—pink and yellow checkerboards on one foot, yellow and white swirls on the other.

"Marcy and Greg," Clara repeats. "They stayed in this cottage last summer."

"Negative," Amber says, taking another tug at her wedge.

"Oh, well, sorry to bother you," Clara says. "I just noticed that people had moved in and thought that maybe you were them."

"Not so fast, my little Avon lady." PJ steps in front of Amber, bumping her out of the way. He unfolds a napkin and throws it down over the threshold, red-carpet-like, to invite Clara in. "You couldn't possibly leave without experiencing my delectables."

"It's not *that* kind of door-to-door," Amber says.

"Don't mind her," PJ says, extending a runny, half-cooked egg sandwich out to Clara. "She's all thorns and bristles. But do indulge yourself in a bite of my delights. I hope you like tartar sauce."

"The only delight you have to offer is a trip down to Beach Blanket Bagel to get us some *real* breakfast," Amber says.

"Bristle bristle, spike spike." He hisses at Amber.

"Hi," I say, in an effort to save the girl from being preyed on by PJ. I introduce everyone, and Clara waves a hello.

"Where are you from?" Drea asks. She fumbles her way off Chad and his newspaper to come and greet her.

"Hartford," Clara says. "But my parents are both from here originally, so we rent a place up here every summer. I've already been here a week."

"Great," Chad says, doing that I-should-be-an-Abercrombie-&-Fitch-model thing with his hair. He threads his fingers through his sandy-brown locks, one strand conveniently landing just to the right of his eye—completely rehearsed. "So you'll be able to fill us in on all the good spots."

Drea pauses a moment to eye the inch of hula-girl tummy peeping out between Clara's T-shirt and sarong. She peeks back at Chad, totally catching him in a gawk.

"Definitely," Clara says, propping her sunglasses up on her head like a makeshift headband. "You guys will *love* vacationing here. Great clubs, cool stores. There's this amazing soda place downtown where they make the best ice-cream floats and frappes and stuff."

"Sounds fattening," Drea says, now scanning the slice of thigh peeping out from Clara's sarong.

"I guess it is," Clara says with a giggle. She pauses to adjust the ties on her sarong—to cover her leg maybe. "But lucky for me, I don't have to worry about that." She glances a moment at Drea's caboose.

"Is there a problem?" Drea asks, obviously noticing the butt check.

"Huh?" Clara cocks her head, feigning innocence.

"Don't mind her," Chad interrupts. "It sounds like a great place."

"Well, we'll have to go," Clara says, with more giggles.

Drea clears her throat. She rests her head on Chad's shoulder and bats her eyes at him. "Let's go for a walk."

"Okay," he says, not moving.

"Now," she says, pouting her strawberry lips at him. "I feel like some beachy air."

Chad obeys, and they leave.

"I think I need some air, too," Amber says. "That and a couple of frat boys to keep me busy. I wonder if they're hungry." She grabs a plateful of Nutella-smothered toast slices.

"They'd have to be starving," PJ says, taking a bite of his egg sandwich.

"What's that supposed to mean?"

"You figure it out." PJ collects a couple more sandwiches from the table and goes off into his room.

"He's just bitter that I won't go out with him again." Amber stuffs a couple tissues into her bikini top, right between her boobs, inside the cleavage. "It gets sweaty down there," she explains. She flashes us a peace-sign good-bye and heads out.

"Wow," Clara says, "I guess I really know how to clear a room."

"Not at all," I say, noticing how Jacob has left as well. I hear the shower valve squeak on in the bathroom and assume that's where he is. "My friends are just a little *eccentric.*"

"Well, I really *would* like to get together some time," Clara says. "I mean, it's hard to meet people up here my own age. It's usually just college kids and they don't normally want to hang out with a fifteen-year-old."

"Well, we kind of *are* college kids," I say. "We just graduated from high school and thought it would be fun to rent a place together for a couple weeks this summer—our reward for surviving the aches and pains of prep school."

"Totally," Clara giggles.

"But you don't look fifteen," I add, noticing how she smells like butterscotch pudding. "I mean, I would have said at least sixteen or seventeen."

"Thanks," Clara beams. "So can I give you my number? Maybe I can give you all a tour later."

"Sure." I hand Clara a napkin and a pen, and she scribbles her number across it—circles with smiley faces for the zeroes.

"So maybe I'll see you around later," she says.

I nod and extend my hand to hers for a shake. And that's when I know. When I feel it. It's like my skin has iced over inside her palm. Like a million tiny ice-needles have just splintered into my veins.

Clara is going to die.

three

Clara tells me she needs to head back to her cottage, and I just stand there, my hand still tingling, still frozen from her touch. There's a part of me that wants to just blurt it all out—what I'm sensing, what I feel in my heart is going to happen to her. But instead my jaw shakes at the thought of the words—how they would sound in the air, just hanging over the two of us like hail-filled clouds. I mean, I don't even know this girl. How am I supposed to tell her that I have this gnawing feeling that she's going to die?

She turns to leave, and I can't hold myself back. "Are you okay?" I ask her.

Her face scrunches up. "Yeah, why?"

"I was just wondering." A huge gulp gets stuck in my throat. "You're here with your parents, you said?"

Clara nods, her face twisted up in confusion.

"That's good," I say, feeling somewhat reassured that she's not alone.

"Oh, yeah, right," she giggles, "vacationing with Mom and Dad . . . let the party begin."

"No, it *is* good." I nod and focus hard on her, wondering if I should say more. But what if I do and she doesn't believe me? Or worse, what if she thinks I'm crazy and never wants to speak to me again?

"Well, I should get going," she says, taking a step back like I've totally weirded her out.

This time I let her go, fearful that saying any more at this point would just ruin everything. I know that I'll have a better chance of sounding convincing if I have more to tell her, if I'm able to reveal something from a nightmare— something that only she would know.

I need to get some sleep.

I change the bloodied sheets on my bed and open up all the windows in the room, hoping the balmy beach air and the salty smell of the ocean will help soothe me to sleep. I crawl between the fresh sheets and pull the amulet from around my neck. It's a tiny emerald-green bottle made out of sea glass and threaded through a silver chain. My mother gave it to me for my birthday. She said it reminded her of me. That really meant a lot. I *do* love it. And the fact that she recognizes my taste—not trying to force her tastes on me by buying me some perfume *she* adores—tells me that she respects who I am and what I believe.

I remove the cork from the bottle and spill a few droplets of the lavender oil onto the tip of my finger. The sweet herbal scent helps to center me a bit, helps prepare me for rest. I dab the oil at the pulse points on my neck, at my forehead, chin, and on both cheeks, and then I pull my dream box from my night table.

It's a smallish wooden box I bought at a flea market at the beginning of the summer—smooth, golden pinewood with a chrome hinge and a matching clasp. I lie back in bed, concentrating on the distant sound of the tide going out— the waves pulling at the rocks, stroking them out to sea. Then I open up the dream box and set it right beside me so I can catch my dreams—so they won't escape my consciousness like they did last night.

*   *   *

I roll over so that my cheek rests against the powdery sand, and notice how the warm breeze seems to hover over me like a blanket. And yet I'm freezing. I tuck myself up into the fetal position and concentrate on the sun beaming down right over me. But it doesn't seem to help. I rub my legs together and feel goosebumps sprouting from my skin.

"Stacey . . ." Someone whispers from behind me. A female voice, I think.

I try to open my eyes, to turn and look, but it's like my eyelids have been sewn shut, like I can't move. I listen harder, but I don't hear anything else—just the tinkling of wind chimes playing somewhere in the distance and the bubbling of the ocean as it tugs at the surf.

I take a deep breath to calm the beating in my chest, and picture the cold air rushing out of my lips in one long and puffy swirl.

"Don't tell anyone," her voice continues.

"Clara?" I want to ask, but it's like I can't speak either. I can feel my lips moving, but nothing's coming out.

"If you tell, I'll know." She's closer now. I can feel her icy breath at the back of my neck.

"If you tell, I'll make you pay."

I go to swat behind me, but it's like I'm literally frozen in place. My teeth chatter, my jaw tremors, and my skin stings from the chill. I listen hard for something else and try to breathe my fear away, but it's almost as if my lungs have filled with ice droplets, making each breath harder, colder, shallower.

After a few seconds, I don't hear anything but the cold—like a long and piercing shriek that screams in my ears. I wonder if she's gone, if she's left me here to freeze to death.

"I'm here, Stacey," she whispers, as though reading my thoughts.

I feel myself start to warm a bit—my breath is less frigid, the shrillness in my ears is more like the tide pushing out. And just over it, over the sound of the waves and the chiming, I can hear her crying. It's coming from somewhere in front of me on the sand, like she's lying down, too. I go to reach out to her, my hand now free to move, and feel something soft, my fingers tugging at her hair, maybe.

"Don't tell," she pleads.

I open my eyes, but it takes me a moment to focus. I can see her now; her back faces me. She's lying on her side as well, I think. But it's so white, almost too bright to see— like a veil that covers her. I strain my eyes and notice a trickling of red. It slides down her back and down the curve of her leg. Like blood.

My body shakes from the cold; it's crawling all over me again.

"Stacey," a voice calls.

I move my lips to answer, but again nothing comes out.

"Stacey—"

It takes me a moment to realize that the voice is different now, deeper.

"Rise and shine, sleeping beauty," he says.

I move my lips once more to answer, but my words are blocked. Something's covering my mouth, cutting off my breath. I gasp and the feeling wakes me up. I open my eyes wide. I'm still in bed, still in my room. And Jacob's hovering over me.

"Are you okay?" he asks, moving his head away. "Why are you so cold?" He pulls the covers over me.

But I can't respond right away. The images of my nightmare are still floating around inside my head; I close the dream box up and flip the clasp shut so my dreams don't have time to escape.

"I didn't mean to startle you," he continues, "but we definitely need to talk."

I nod and try to control my breath, concentrating a moment on the puffs as they exhale out my mouth—to see if they're visible from the cold. But they aren't, even though my body's still shaking, still frigid. "I had another nightmare."

"About what?"

I clench my teeth to stop the chattering and, instead of answering, move over to the open window. The ocean is rolling away, stroking at the rocks, leaving a long stretch of beach. I look around, almost half expecting to see Clara out there somewhere. But she isn't—just a couple joggers, a group doing yoga, and a handful of power-walkers. I focus up toward the clouds, trying my best to picture something soothing in their globlike formation—the moon, the sun, a giant butterfly. Anything to try and shake this feeling—this darkness that sits so heavy in my heart. But instead I just see redness, blotches of color that swirl inside my head and funk me up even more.

"Can you tell me about it?" Jacob gets up from the bed and places his hands on my shoulders from behind.

I turn around to face him, just as a trickle of blood rolls off my lip.

four

Jacob pulls off his T-shirt and hands it to me as a tissue. "Thanks," I say, pressing it against my nose, breathing in his familiar lemongrass scent.

"Can we talk about it?" he asks. "The nosebleeds . . . the nightmares."

I nod and take a deep breath, my fingers resting over the dream box.

"Are they in there?" he asks, gesturing toward the box.

"What?"

"Your dreams?"

I feel a slight smile curl up on my face as I remember how he's the one who taught me about dream boxes. I flip the box open. "It was a nightmare," I say, "not a dream."

"And what was it about?"

I turn around to face him, his bare chest now a deep caramel color from the sun. His normally tawny complexion is darker as well, like even though we've been vacationing together for the past three days, it's the first time I'm noticing it. Noticing how his lips look a little bit paler against his tan, smooth skin; how strands of his dark walnut-brown hair look almost golden from the sun; and how his slate-blue eyes seem just a little bit brighter, almost silvery. "Clara," I say, finally. "The girl who came over this morning. That's who I dreamt about." I blot my nose with his T-shirt to make sure the bleeding has stopped.

"So what happened in the dream?"

"I saw her body, I think."

"You think?"

"It was sort of blurred." I close my eyes to try and picture it. "It was so white—almost too white to see. But then everything turned red."

"*Red?*"

I nod. "Like blood. Like she's bleeding."

"Are you sure it was her?"

"I *know* it was her. It was her voice. She told me not to tell." I feel weird just saying the words, like the words themselves are a secret.

"She told you not to tell *what?*" Jacob asks.

I shake my head, remembering how she also told me that if I said anything she'd make me pay. But pay how? "It was a premonition," I say. "I know it was. Something's going to happen to her."

"And the nosebleeds are a clue?"

I nod and glance down at the bloodstained shirt, having to remind myself of how well Jacob knows me. I mean, it just never ceases to amaze me—how much we can sense about each other.

"I felt it, too," I say. "When I shook her hand earlier, I sensed right away that she was in danger."

"So we'll deal with it. We'll figure it out."

"It's starting again," I whisper.

Jacob squeezes my hand, his silvery-blue eyes zooming right into me, turning my insides to mush, making my heart do that pitter-patter thing you read about in one of those glossy pink romance books. I look away to keep focused.

"We'll deal with it," he repeats.

"I know. It's just—I thought this was going to be a relaxing summer."

He pulls something from the pocket of his shorts and places it into my palm. Right away I know what it is. I can tell from the weight, the smooth, rounded edges, and the sheer familiarity of it. My insides start to mush again, my heart swelling up inside my chest. I open my hand to look. The chunky rocklike crystal fits just perfectly in my palm.

"You left it in my room the other night," he says. "I sensed you might need it right about now."

"Sensed?"

Jacob nods and looks away. That's when it hits me, when I sense it too—he's obviously having nightmares as well. I wait for him to tell me about them, but he just keeps silent.

"How did you know I might need the crystal?" I ask.

"Easy," he says. "Because I know you."

"You're having them too, aren't you?"

"What?"

"Nightmares."

He wipes away the stray strand of dark hair that has fallen over his eye. "No," he says, looking away.

But I know he isn't telling the truth. Jacob and I have a connection that's stronger than anything I've ever experienced. In fact, we couldn't be more alike. We've both been brought up with folk magic, and we both experience premonitions. They're actually what brought us together.

Last year, Jacob was having nightmares that someone was going to kill me. Only he didn't even know who I was. He just knew he was having premonitions about some girl who was going to die. After doing some research and honing in on his senses, he ended up transferring schools to find me, practically three thousand miles away. The next thing I knew, here was this guy, this *stranger*, trying to save my life. Except he never quite felt like a stranger. Sometimes I feel like I can look at him and know exactly what he's thinking. Like right now.

"I don't know why you're not being honest with me," I say.

"It's not what you're thinking," he says.

"You're *not* having nightmares?"

"Not about Clara."

"Then what?" I ask. *"Tell me."*

"Not now," he says. "Right now, we should focus on *your* nightmares. Mine are nothing I can't handle." He takes my hand and sandwiches it between his palms. "Trust me."

"I do."

"Good." He kisses my cheek and brings his lips up to my ear. "I love you," he whispers.

I smile and look away, wanting to tell him that I love him too. But I can't. I just can't seem to get those three little words out, even though I feel them in my heart. And I don't know why. I mean, I *have* said it before—to friends, to family—just not to him. With him it's different; it's true love—the real thing, the till-death-do-us-part kind. And for some reason, even though I try to show him I love him all the time, the actual words get stuck in my throat.

"Say something," he says.

"Like what?"

"Like what you're thinking."

"The same thing you are," I say coyly.

Jacob smiles and bites his lower lip, staring down at my mouth, making my cheeks feel all warm and flushed. I know he must notice that I don't say it.

"Maybe we should talk about something else," I say.

"Right," he says, straightening up. "We should talk about your nightmares more."

"No," I say. "I mean, let's talk about something else entirely."

"Why?"

"Because," I say, scrunching my knees in toward my chest, "maybe for five measly minutes I'd just like to be normal."

five

Jacob leaves so I can try and get some sleep, so I can dream and have another nightmare. But as much as I try, even after breaking out brand-new bottles of patchouli and lavender oils, after stuffing a vanilla-bean dream bag under my pillow, it just doesn't work. I'm so completely awake it's pathetic.

Instead of sulking over my lack of sleep, I spend some time meditating on Clara—on her name, her butterscotch scent, and the way my hand felt when she touched it. The rest of my day is spent at the beach with the gang, playing volleyball and eating clam chowder from bread bowls. Every so often I remind myself of Clara. I even cap my night off by inking a giant capital *C* on my hand to encourage Clara-specific dreams. All of this makes me think that when I wake up in the morning I'll have enough insightful info so she'll simply *have* to believe me.

But, once again, I barely sleep at all. I end up tossing and turning in bed all night, even waking up Amber and Drea a couple times.

As soon as I feel myself start to nod off, the tightness in my chest, like piano wire, reminds me how stressed I am, how much there is at stake. I mean, if I don't figure all of this out, Clara could seriously die—just like Veronica Leeman, almost two years ago now; just like Maura, three years before that. The premonitions I'd had involving them had been telling but, in Maura's case, I ignored the nightmares and they came true. In Veronica's case, I wasn't able to figure everything out in time. The result—two girls dead, and me scared to death that another might die.

I press my eyes closed and roll over in bed, thinking how this is just like what happened to Jacob last year, how he was having premonitions about a stranger—me—but he still felt compelled to put his life to the side and help. And what if he hadn't? Would I even be here right now?

I have to help Clara; there's really no other choice.

As a result, I've decided to start early this morning. I grab a few spell supplies and head out for a walk. I just need to be alone right now, though the throngs of people starting to fill up the beach despite the early hour, dragging their towels, beach chairs, and coolers full of soda onto the sand, is making that a bit difficult. Still, I keep close to the water, trudging along through the wet sand as it tugs at my feet, trying to concentrate on the lapping of the water and not the voices of the tourists all around me.

I keep hearing that other voice, though. Clara's voice, warning me not to tell. But tell who? Or what?

The icy feeling returns to my fingers just thinking about Clara. I do my best to shake it off, but it just won't let me go. The chill travels up my arm and over my shoulder, hugging around the right side of my neck. It must be at least eighty-five degrees out here, but still I pull my sweater tightly around me in fear of icing over completely.

When I feel I've gotten far enough away from the clusters of people, I sink down into the wet sand and breathe the salt air in, doing my best to calm this nervous feeling inside me. I look up toward the sun, knowing that if I focus enough on its energy, I'll be able to concentrate on what's important.

Clara. I repeat her name over and over again and then write it out in the thick, wet sand with my finger. I picture the sun's rays beaming down over her name and over me, opening up the channels of clear thought. And it works, to a point—my hand, arm, and neck are a little less tingly, less cold.

From the pocket of my sweater I grab the few spell supplies I've brought along—an old perfume bottle I've been saving, a purple pen, and a slip of paper. The bottle has been bathed in the moonlight, left on my windowsill for two complete moon cycles. I remove its cork and position it on the sand before me, imagining the warm ocean air filtering in through the mouth; the heat of the sun, like fire, washing over the glass. I uncap the purple pen and, on the slip of paper, write the words DON'T TELL ANYONE, hoping the purple color will help promote psychic awareness.

I slip the paper into the bottle and top it off with elements of earth and water—a palmful of saltwater from the ocean and a sprinkling of sand from the beach. I cork the bottle and hold it out to the wind. "O Spirit, Spirit, I beg of thee to help me see with clarity. I offer you earth, wind, and sea, and pray that you will answer me." I kiss the bottle and then throw it out into the ocean as far as my strength will allow. It collides with a wave and gets swallowed up for a couple seconds, but then it bobs its way back up to the surface. The incoming tide pushes the bottle toward my feet. I throw it out again, harder this time, but it comes back just the same. Instead of plucking it out of the water, I decide to just let the bottle swim along with the incoming tide. Maybe instead of relying so heavily upon my spells, I should trust my instincts more. Right now my instincts are telling me that I need to find Clara.

Six

I distinctly remember Clara mentioning that her place is a few houses down from ours—to the left, I think.

There's a cottage to the left that looks pretty tame—beach chairs stacked neatly on the porch, a portable grill tucked away in the corner, seashell-shaped wind chimes hanging down over the stairs. I'm thinking this is the place since I also remember her saying that she's here with her parents and not a flock of beer-guzzling fraternity boys. It appears as though the frat guys have taken up at least three or four of the houses to the right of us.

I climb the stairs and knock on the door. It creaks open slightly from the impact, like it wasn't quite closed. I hold it shut and try knocking again.

Still no response.

"Hello?" I call into the door crack. The seashell wind chimes jingle just behind me, forcing me to remember that I heard the same sound in my nightmare. "Clara?" I call, edging the door open a bit wider.

I close my eyes a moment and concentrate on the jingling. But then I hear something else. It's coming from inside—a high-pitched, beeping sound. I push the door open farther. "Clara? Are you in here?"

It's dark in the living room; all the shades are pulled down. There's a clamoring noise coming from one of the rooms, like someone's struggling with something. I open the door even wider and take a step inside, noticing that the layout of this cottage is exactly like ours. The living room and kitchen are connected, like one big open area. I move toward the short, narrow hallway and the bedrooms that branch off it.

But now it's just quiet. And dark—the only light available is what's coming in through the door I entered, and the farther I get away from it, the darker it gets. I peer over my shoulder at the door, thinking how maybe I should go and get help, but all I can focus on are those stupid wind chimes—and the thought that Clara might be in trouble. I call her name yet again.

Still no response.

I move toward the bedroom to the right and place my ear up to the door. But it's just quiet, all except for my heart; it's pounding hard inside my chest. I place my hand over the doorknob, half thinking that it's going to be locked, but instead it turns. And I go in.

It's even darker in here—too dark to see. I feel over the walls for a light switch, but can't seem to find one. I move toward the center of the room, my arms outstretched, and end up tripping over something hard, a footstool maybe.

A loud cracking sound comes from out in the living room, like the front door has been shut. But maybe it's just the wind. I bite the inside of my cheek and tell myself this is so, that the breezy ocean air drew the door closed, that no one's here, that in a few seconds I can just sneak back out.

But then I hear footsteps, the sound of floorboards creaking in this direction. I stand behind the door and hold my breath to keep from gasping out.

"Hello?" whispers a male voice, one I don't recognize.

I close my eyes and try to picture myself someplace else.

"Come on out," he sings. "I don't bite."

I clench my teeth and ball myself up in the corner just as the light in the room flicks on, making everything red. I look up toward the ceiling at the red light bulb that shines down over what is obviously a darkroom. There's a clothesline hung at the back of the room with pictures attached to it, a large workstation set up with bins for solutions, and racks lining the walls.

I can hear him breathing from the other side of the door. Clutching the crystal and willing Jacob's strength to assist me, I close my eyes and silently count to twenty, praying that he won't come all the way in, that he'll close the door back up and go. I peer around the room for a window. There's one in the far corner, but it looks as though it's been boarded up.

The light flicks off a few seconds later and he leaves, just like that, drawing the door closed behind him. I wait a few seconds, listening at the wall as his footsteps travel down the hallway and into the living room. And then I hear the front door slam closed as though he's left.

I leave too. I get up, open the door just enough to allow me through, and move down the hallway as quickly and quietly as possible. I go to the living room door, but the knob won't turn. I twist the lock until it clicks and try the door again. Still locked.

"Where are you going so soon?" a voice asks from just behind me.

I turn around. He's standing just a few feet away, but it's still so dark. The only light is coming in through the kitchen window.

"We haven't even met," he continues.

He's older, maybe thirty or fortyish, with a face full of hair—a thick and wiry honey-colored beard and a moustache that sticks out on both sides.

"I have to go. I'm so sorry. I've made a mistake." My jaw is shaking.

"Let me help you." He stretches his arms and lets out a giant yawn, like he just woke up.

"I was just looking for someone. I've made a mistake," I repeat.

"Who?" he asks, taking a step closer toward me. He's wearing a pair of paint-splattered jeans with an old and ratty T-shirt.

"No one." My hands behind my back, I try turning the lock the other way. I pull the knob, but it still doesn't budge.

"Trick lock," he says, smiling at me. He grabs at his facial hair, giving it a good tug. "Stay a while. Let me take your picture." He moves over to the sofa to grab his camera just as I pull on the knob and turn the lock, remembering how that's the way the trick lock works at my aunt's house.

It works. The doorknob twists, enabling me to open it, to fly out the door and down the steps.

When I get a safe distance away, I turn to glance back. He's still standing there, still watching me.

seven

I boot it down the beach strip, eager to get away from him—from his stare and the way he made me feel, like a victim waiting to happen.

My heart is still hammering; all I can think about is what would have happened if I didn't get out, what he would have done. Needless to say, it probably wasn't a good idea that I went in there in the first place. It's just that those wind chimes, the sound of them jingling just behind me on the porch, reminded me so much of my nightmare.

When I feel I've gotten far enough away, I stop to catch my breath, to roll my shoulders back and remind myself that I need to find Clara. I've practically walked this entire beach strip with the full intention of looking for her, but I haven't been looking at all.

I take a deep breath and start to backtrack toward our cottage, keeping focused the whole time. There are tons of people sunning themselves on the beach. But I don't see Clara anywhere.

"Hey, sexy girlfriend," a voice shouts toward me.

Amber.

I look up and see her piggybacking one of the frat guys around on their back porch; it looks like her legs could snap off at any moment.

"I am *so* glad to see you," I shout, heading over to join them.

"Rough morning?" she asks.

"The roughest."

"Details?"

"Later," I say, noticing how Frat Boy is hovering, quite literally, over her shoulder.

"Hey there," he says, extending a leg toward me as though I'm supposed to shake it. "I'm Sully."

"And I'm Stacey," I say, looking at the scab on his knee, deciding that the last thing I want to do is touch his sweaty skin.

"That's Casey over there." Sully points with his foot to the guy sitting on the ground in the corner, drinking from a cozy and looking off toward the beach. I didn't even notice him there. Though it doesn't appear as though he notices me either. He hasn't looked up from the beach once. I peer in the same direction to see what he's hawking at. As if I needed to ask.

It's Drea. She and Chad have set up camp at the shoreline, complete with beach blanket, cooler, and tilty umbrella. They're goading each other to jump into the water—Drea in a two-piece, stringy number and Chad in a pair of swim trunks that go down to his knees.

"So," Amber says, practically beaming like a kagillion-watt bulb, "notice anything?"

"What?"

"Double trouble."

"Huh?" I feel my face curl up in cluelessness.

"Or double the fun—depending how you look at it."

"Um, what are you talking about?"

"Sully and Casey are twins." She's practically birthday-party clapping now.

I look back and forth at the two guys—brownish hair, dark eyes, round faces, same slender build with long, wiry legs.

"Isn't that the coolest?" she gleams.

Absolutely thrilling, I think to myself. I nod and fake a smile in an effort to feign enthusiasm.

"There's an overnight cruise Thursday night. One of their frat brother's fathers owns a party-cruise company."

"It's a fundraiser," Sully explains. "The boat will leave at night, anchor for a few hours, and then we'll be back by morning."

"And it's only a hundred bucks per room," she continues. "If we all pool our money . . ."

"We've capped it off at four per room."

Amber arches her eyebrows, probably doing the math, probably picturing herself finding alternative sleeping arrangements. But since I hardly feel like arguing with her about some overnight frat-boy drink-fest, I nod a few more seconds, waiting for the moment to pass. "So have any of you seen that Clara girl around here?" I ask.

"Clara?" Casey perks up.

"Yeah, you know her?" I ask.

"Not really," he says. "Why are you looking for her?"

"Because I want to talk to her." I can hear a twinge of irritation in my voice.

"Why?"

Why? Try none of your freaking business. I stifle the thought with yet another plastic smile.

"She was around here a little while ago, but then she took off." Casey looks back out toward the beach.

"He *made* her go," Sully says.

"I didn't make anyone go anywhere."

"Telling her to get lost is a funny way to show it."

"Whatever," Casey says, taking another sip from his cozy. "I'm just sick of her always trying to hang on us."

Okay, more confusion. Cute Girl who likes to hang on obviously Dateless Guy equals irritation to the point where Dateless Guy makes Cute Girl leave? What's wrong with this equation?

Casey gets up and goes into the house, slamming the door shut behind him.

"What's with him?" Amber asks, letting Sully down off her back. She stumbles around on the porch like the Hunchback of Notre Dame, though I'm not so sure she's kidding.

"He's just got his panties caught in a wedge."

"I hate it when that happens." Amber picks at her own wedge.

"No," Sully says. "I mean, his girlfriend broke up with him a few days ago."

"So what does that have to do with Clara?" I ask.

"Oh wow," Amber says. "That's really sad—his girlfriend broke up with him right in the middle of swimsuit season . . ." She shakes her head and purses her lips, feigning the picture of grief. "So I take it you're both without girlfriends?"

Oh so subtle.

Sully doesn't reply. He just looks out at the beach, toward Drea, now rubbing tanning oil onto her mist-on-tanned legs. "I should go talk to Casey," Sully says.

"And I should go talk to Clara," I say.

"Who am I gonna talk to?" Amber pouts.

"Try the Clam Stripper," Sully says to me. He points down the length of the beach. "I think Clara sometimes hangs out there."

"Wait," I say, "you didn't answer my question."

"What question?"

"What does Casey's breakup have to do with Clara?"

"Look, I'm not saying anything, all right?"

"Well, you sort of already did," I volley back.

"Look, I just think she's the kind of girl who can start problems."

"Because she's a flirt?"

"Because she likes to take other girls' guys."

"Well, I guess we're okay then," Amber says, "'cause we don't have other girls' guys to take."

I turn to look at her—her face completely serious despite her mishmash of logic. "I'm leaving," I say, already halfway down the stairs.

"Wait," Amber calls after me. "Can I come? I could *so* eat."

"Only if you promise not to talk. I just really need to think right now."

"This is a *vacation*, Stacey. You're not *supposed* to think. Save it for September."

"Right," I say. "Because that's your motto."

"No way. Thinking is way overrated. I prefer to just feel."

"And what are you feeling right now?"

"Sheer and utter elation," she says. "I just scored myself a date with a set of twins."

"Yeah, but do *they* know that?"

"Not yet," she says. "But they will."

eight

Drea, ticked off at Chad for some unknown reason, sees Amber and me hiking it down to the Clam Stripper and decides to join us.

"So what did he do?" Amber asks her. "Forget to compliment you on your tan?"

"I don't want to talk about it."

"Because I'm right?"

"Because I refuse to discuss my grown-up relationship with someone who still hasn't outgrown comic-book heroes." Drea pauses to gaze at Amber's Superwoman swim shorts and at the enormous gold *S* spandexed across her chest.

"This from a girl who still pouts to get what she wants," Amber says.

"Can you guys just stop?" I ask. "I'm sort of having a bad day and your negative energy is funking me up even more."

"Why?" Drea asks. "What happened?"

"I really don't feel like getting into it right now. Later, okay?"

"Somebody's PMSing," Amber says.

"A little compassion, please?" I ask.

"I meant me," Amber says.

"Look," I say, taking a big breath. "All I'm saying is that this is my field trip to the Clam Stripper, and I expect you both to behave, or you'll have to wait inside the bus."

"I wish we *had* taken a bus." Amber starts trudging along the beach like she's got weights strapped to her ankles. "I mean, could this sand be any heavier? It's way too much of a workout on the legs."

"Maybe you shouldn't have piggybacked Frat Boy," I say.

"*Those* pipe-cleaner legs supported a two-hundred-pound college boy?" Drea asks.

"Maybe you should stop worrying about my lack of muscle and focus on your abundance of jiggle," Amber says, glancing down at Drea's thighs.

"*Excuse me?*" Drea asks.

"You heard me."

Drea stops mid-step and starts shimmying her hips from side to side. "I dare you to find even one ounce of jiggle."

"Drea," I say, blocking the view of some grandpa who's taking a serious liking to her rump. He reaches over into his beach bag for a pair of eyeglasses. "Be serious. You know she's just joking."

"Are you?" Drea asks, her lips budding up in a scowl.

Amber shrugs, takes one last jabbing peek in the direction of Drea's butt, and raises an eyebrow.

"You guys are so rude to each other," I say. "Sometimes I don't even know how you two stay friends."

"Oh, come on, Stace," Amber says. "We're rude to you, too. I hope you don't feel left out."

"Unfortunately not."

"But you know my verbal stingers are only poisoned with love," she continues.

"Love?"

"Yeah, you know it's all harmless." Amber smacks a big fat kiss on my cheek, then turns and does the same to Drea. "I mean, I love you guys. It's how I show it."

"Yeah, but do you have to show it so *well?*" Drea asks.

The Clam Stripper is just up ahead. It's basically this grilled-food place with an adjoining deck where people eat and lots of picnic tables that are set up on the sand. There's a sexified giant plastic clam that stands high atop the roof of the place. One shell is clutched at her front like a towel; the other is swung high above her head as though she's about to toss it out to the crowd.

"So why *do* you want to talk to Clara?" Amber asks.

"*Who?*" Drea pauses to look at me.

"Clara," I say. "The girl who stopped by yesterday morning."

"The sarong?" Drea takes a moment to straighten out the straps on her bikini, to run a finger over her lipgloss, and to push her hair forward on her shoulders.

"Exactly," I say.

"So why do you want to talk to *her?*"

"You really want to know?"

"Um, yeah," Drea says, still checking herself over, "that's why I asked."

"I had a nightmare about her."

"Excuse me?" Drea gasps.

"Not a-freakin'-gain," Amber says.

"It's true."

"How do you know?" Drea stops us, turning me around to face her.

"The blood," Amber shouts. She takes a step back and covers her mouth. "I knew it . . . the blood bath yesterday morning. It's a clue, right?"

"What is wrong with you?" Drea asks her.

I look around at the attention Amber's caused; one woman pulls her toddler close, a look of horror stamped on her face, as though we might hurt him.

"Come on," I say. "Let's go. We'll talk about this later."

"No way," Amber says. "We need to talk about it now. We need a strategy."

"What you need is to keep quiet for five minutes." I take a deep breath and resume our walk, mentally cursing myself for thinking I could tell them outside the confines of our room.

"I'm actually surprised we didn't think of it sooner," Drea says. "I mean, it's not exactly normal for your nose to bleed . . . especially like that."

"Yeah, but why *would* you think of it?" I say. "I mean, noses *do* bleed, especially in dry weather. And it has been nine whole months since I've had side effects from nightmares."

"Plus," Amber says, "what are we supposed to think? That every time you get the runs or have extra-bad period cramps that something bad is going to happen?"

"Wait," Drea says, as though it's just dawned on her. She tugs at my arm to stop us again. "Are you seriously trying to tell me that some random girl shows up at our place and now you're having nightmares about her? That's completely messed."

"No," I say, "what's messed is that you don't believe me. After everything."

"I'm just asking questions here, Stacey. I mean, don't you think it's a little convenient? The girl you happened to be dreaming about shows up at our door?"

"What are you saying?"

"I'm not saying anything; I'm just trying to understand."

"Okay, fine." I take another full breath. "I know it sounds crazy, but yesterday, when I shook her hand, I sensed right away that she was in danger."

"So it wasn't a nightmare," Amber says.

"No," I say, "it was. It was both. I *had* both."

Drea studies my face for a few moments. "You're really serious, aren't you?"

"Of course I'm serious. How could I joke about something like this?"

"You couldn't," she says. "That's *why* I believe you." She rubs my forearm. "Just tell me how I can help."

"Me too," Amber says, picking her wedge for the umpteenth time today.

"Just be there for me—when I need to de-stress."

"No stressing out allowed," Amber says.

"At least not without friends like Ben & Jerry." Drea wraps her arm around me.

"Um, excuse me," Amber says, "but last I checked our names were Drea and Amber."

"Hopeless," Drea says, rolling her eyes.

I can't help but giggle in agreement.

*　　*　　*

When we get to the restaurant, I look up toward the deck area and see Clara right away. She's sitting alone at a table, nursing a frappe. We climb the steps to the food counter area and she notices us right away. She pauses from frappe-sipping and waves us over.

"Do you want us to come?" Drea asks.

"Of course she does," Amber says, scoping out the trays full of food that collect at the pick-up window beside us.

"I don't know," I say. "Maybe I should go alone."

"You're actually going to tell her?" Drea asks. "Just like that? I mean, how are you even going to say it?"

"Easy," Amber says, nabbing a fry off someone's plate. "'Excuse me, Clara,'" she mimics, "'but I had this incredibly horrible nightmare about you and, well, I have reason to believe that you're going to die.' Stace, do we have any time frame on the death?"

I shake my head.

"I think we should come," Drea says. "At least me." She pauses to evil-eye Amber. "I've been through this before. I know what it's like to be the victim. I might be able to help ease her."

"Oh, and I *can't?*" Amber pipes. She snatches a fried clam strip off somebody's tray and pops it into her mouth. "I'm the queen of ease."

"Yeah, that's what they say."

"Time out," I say, clutching Jacob's crystal, still in my pocket. I close my eyes for just a moment to breathe the sun's energy in—focusing on its ability to enlighten and empower. "Let's all go."

nine

Clara seems absolutely thrilled to have us join her at the table. I don't think her smile could get any wider or more contagious. She's sitting on the edge of the bench, practically bouncing up and down in pure delight.

So how am I supposed to tell her what I have to say?

"I'm so excited to see you guys," she beams. "Are you eating? Can I treat you to a frappe or some French fries?"

"Free food?" Amber says, peering up at the menu board. "I'm so in. I'll take a super-sized Chocolicious and a mega-bucket of onion rings, please."

"Get it yourself," Drea says.

"Who died and made you Queen B?" Amber asks. "No wonder you and Chad are fighting."

"I didn't say we were fighting," Drea says. "We just got into a little argument."

"Oh, really?" Clara's eyes widen. "The blond guy, right? He's super cute."

"Um . . . thanks," Drea says, furrowing her eyebrows at the compliment. "I'm sure he'll be ready to apologize by the time I get back."

"Anyway—" I begin.

"Anyway," Clara interrupts. "I know what it's like to have boy problems. I was seeing this guy who was really, really nice at first. We went to all these fun places together—out to eat, to the movies, downtown. But then all this stuff happened, and he told me that he didn't want to see me anymore."

"Sounds like a weenie," Amber says, eyeing the hotdog traveling by on somebody's tray. "Okay, I seriously need to snack. Anybody want anything?"

We shake our heads, and Amber heads over to the order window.

"So," I say, in an effort to steer the conversation back to where I want it. "I think there's something we really need to talk about."

"Oh my god," Clara says, looking toward the order window. "There she is."

"Who?" Drea turns to look. There's a girl standing behind Amber in line. She's got jet-black hair with thick auburn highlights and deeply tan skin, like melted cocoa.

"That guy I was talking about, the one I was seeing . . . that's his ex."

"So . . ." Drea says, eyeing the girl's style, maybe—the way she's completely color-coordinated. Her tangerine-colored flip-flops match her bathing suit, sunglasses, *and* the watch around her wrist.

"So she's the reason we're not together," Clara says. "He never told me he had a girlfriend, so then when she found us out, she got all wacko and went completely ballistic."

"Ballistic how?" I ask, looking back at the girl, wondering if she might be the real threat.

"Totally nuts," Clara explains. "She freaked at him, at me . . . I mean, she totally blew things out of proportion."

"I don't know," Drea says. "God help the poor boy who cheats on me. Your guy sounds like a jerk."

"I guess," Clara says, sipping her frappe. "But I miss him. We're supposed be going on a cruise together in a couple days."

"His name wouldn't happen to be Casey?" I ask, realizing how familiar all of this sounds.

"Yeah," Clara nods. "You know him? Did he say anything about me?"

Clara's eyes are all wide and concerned, like this is really important to her. I concentrate on her face a moment, at her trembling lips—like she could lose it at any moment—and the ashen tone that seems to hover all around her.

"Not really," I say, remembering how angry Casey got over the mere mention of Clara.

"Look at how she's staring at me," Clara says, looking back at Casey's ex. "Like it's all my fault."

"Clara," I demand, nabbing her attention back. "You need to listen to me. What I'm about to say is going to sound a little crazy."

"But Stacey can help you," Drea says. "I mean, she helped me."

"Oh my god," Clara says. "Is it something Casey said? Something he told you?"

"It's not about Casey," I say, feeling a chill pass over my shoulders. "At least I don't think it is."

Clara cocks her head like I've confused her even more.

"It's about you," I say, taking a giant breath. "I had a nightmare about you."

"Excuse me?" Her eyebrows arch as though I've caught her off guard—as though she's stuck somewhere between surprised and confused.

"You need to trust Stacey," Drea says. "I know this sounds crazy, but she sees things in her dreams—her nightmares—and the stuff comes true. It happened a couple years ago with me. Stacey was having nightmares that some guy was going to try and kill me. And the nightmares came true."

"But you're still sitting here."

"Because of Stacey," Drea continues. "Because she was able to predict the future before it happened—so we could stop it."

"Right," Clara says. She's nodding her head, looking back and forth at the two of us, probably wondering who's more crazy.

"Just hear me out," I say. "Please."

She folds her arms and looks away, toward Casey's ex again, now sitting at one of the picnic tables. She and her friend notice Clara and start talking amongst themselves, letting out a couple obnoxious squeals loud enough for us to hear. They look back over at us and Clara looks away.

"Clara," I say, "are you listening to me?"

"Sure." She giggles. "You were saying something about your nightmares?"

I nibble the inside of my cheek, wondering how I can put this, how I can soften it in some way. But then I just say it: "You're in trouble. Serious trouble."

Clara nods at me, biting down on her lower lip, as though she's holding in a laugh.

"It's not a joke," I say. "Has everything in your life been going normal?"

"Normal?"

"I mean, has anything different happened to you?"

"Different how?"

I shake my head, trying to think of something else to say, something that might lead me to an answer. "Is there something you don't want to tell anyone?"

"Like what?" She laughs.

"I don't know," I say, remembering the voice in my dream. "Is there something you don't want other people to know?"

I feel stupid even asking these questions—like she'd ever tell me, a complete stranger, her most intimate secrets. I take a deep breath, thinking how my grandmother always knew how to ask just the right questions, how none of her questions were ever too pointed, and how they always encouraged the fullest, most telling answers—like she was able to sense what people wanted to talk about. So why can't I do the same?

"It's really no big deal," Clara says. "I sometimes have creepy nightmares, too. But nothing freaky happens. It was probably just like that."

"No," I say, "it's different for me. My nightmares come true."

"Why don't you tell Clara what she was doing in your nightmare," Drea suggests. "You know, like, was she running? Was she hiding? Was she doing anything unusual or significant?"

"Well," I grimace, "I didn't exactly see her in my nightmare."

"Um, *what?*" Drea's mouth falls open.

I sigh, completely frustrated with myself, with how I sound. "I know it doesn't make sense. But you have to trust me. I heard Clara's voice in my dream; I'm sure of it."

"And what did my voice say?" Clara asks.

"You told me not to tell anyone." I wait a couple moments for her response, to see if the words from my nightmare might conjure up some memory—inspire her to tell me something significant. But she looks completely dumfounded—her mouth hanging open, as though waiting for me to finish my thought.

"I told you not to tell anyone *what?*" she asks.

"That's just it," I say. "I don't know."

"Wow," she says, with a giggle, as though I'm certifiably whacko. "That's really weird. I don't know what to say."

"Look," I say, leaning in closer, "something significant is going to happen to you—something that might be . . . not exactly good. So, if it's okay with you—even if it isn't okay with you—I'm going to be looking out for you."

"Sounds great," she beams. "I mean, it'll be fun to hang out; it can get pretty dull around here."

"Onion ring, anyone?" Amber interrupts the awkward moment, smacking her tray down on the table. It's piled high with just about every artery-clogging snack the strip joint must be serving up today—fried clams, onion rings, a couple hot dogs, and four super-sized Chocoliciouses. "Couldn't decide what to eat, so I just figured I'd order one of all my craves." She sets the frappes down in front of us. "So what did I miss?"

"Stacey was just trying to explain to Clara about her nightmares, how they come true."

"Yeah," Amber says, pointing at Clara with an onion ring. "So, you gotta listen to her or else you'll end up fertilizing dandelions."

"Amber—" I snap.

"So much for the queen of ease." Drea sighs.

"Try one of these, will you?" Amber says, completely oblivious to her lack of subtlety. She stuffs her mouth full of fried clam. "They seem a little sandy to me."

Clara grabs one and starts chewing away. I can't tell if she's nervous or hungry or merely looking for a diversion.

"So what do you think?" Amber asks.

"About the clams?" Clara asks.

"About everything."

"I vote not to think." She grabs another clam strip.

"Finally," Amber says, "someone who sees things the same way I do."

"A scary thought," Drea says, taking an onion ring.

I dive in to the greasy treats as well. Perhaps we could all use a little thoughtless diversion—for at least a little while anyway.

ten

When I get back to the cottage, Jacob is in the kitchen unpacking grocery bags.

"Hi," I say, shutting the door behind me.

He pauses from unpacking, a bunch of fresh carrots dangling from his grip. "Are you all right?"

I shrug.

"Where is everybody?" he asks.

"Amber and Drea decided to go for a swim, and I think I might have seen Chad and PJ playing volleyball with some of the frat guys from next door. How come you're not out, too?" I ask. "The water's seventy degrees—practically spa conditions."

"Didn't feel like it." He comes around the side of the counter to greet me. He takes my hands, nuzzles his forehead against mine, and looks straight into my eyes—all of which under normal circumstances would turn my knees to absolute jelly. But today I'm feeling oppressively rigid. "It's just you and me."

"Yeah," I say, managing a smile.

"What's wrong?"

"Where do I begin?"

"I take it you talked to Clara," he says.

"That's just a fraction of my freak-show morning."

"What do you mean?"

I proceed to tell him about my accidental encounter with the creepy photographer guy from next door and then I segue into my conversation-turned-pigout-fest with Clara. "She probably thinks I'm crazy."

"It doesn't really matter what she thinks," he says. "All that matters is you're going to help her."

"I know."

"Then what?"

"I guess I'm just feeling really stressed."

Jacob folds me up into his arms where it feels safe, and kisses my ear, and whispers that everything will be okay, that we'll get through this together. And I know that should make me feel better, but for some reason his super self-confidence is completely bugging me.

"Just promise me one thing," he says. "No more breaking into the darkrooms of creepy photographers, you hear me? At least not without me by your side."

"Deal," I say, breaking the embrace. "I think maybe I just need to lie down for a bit."

"Want some company?"

I shake my head.

"Well, can I at least make you some iced tea?"

More head shaking, even though the thought of raspberry tea over ice sounds so completely heavenly right now. "I just want to take a nap." I give Jacob an icy peck on the lips and head into the bedroom, feeling the windchill off my back plummet the temperature in the room from eighty degrees to ten below zero.

I close the bedroom door and press my back up against it, feeling like I've plucked the Queen B crown right off Drea's head and propped it high atop mine. That's when I notice the cream-colored vase by my bed and the thick bunch of fresh white lilacs gathered inside, making me feel even worse.

I'm just about to turn and go back into the kitchen, to serve Jacob my special of the day—grovel cake, complete with two cups of apology and a half-dozen kisses—when I hear a knock at the door. I turn to open it.

It's Jacob. He's balancing a tray in one hand, waiter-style. He comes into the room and sets the tray down on my night table, a tall frosted glass of raspberry tea perched in the center. "I had a feeling you might want some anyway."

"You know me way too well." I wrap my arms around him and kiss his neck, wanting more than anything to whisper into his ear how much he means to me, how much I truly, madly love him. But instead I just say, "Thank you for the flowers. They're beautiful."

"Not to mention a certain person's favorite brand of cookies."

I look down at the plate of Mallomars and topple him over the bed, planting not six, not seven, but at least *ten* whopping kisses across his lips, topping them off with a feature-film-worthy make-out scene.

"Wow," he says, when the kisses break. "I should have brought you tea and cookies ages ago. What'll I get if I bring you a hot fudge sundae?"

"Very funny," I say, sitting up. Aside from the tea and cookies, he's also brought a couple bottles of oil extracts. "Lemongrass and jasmine?"

"So your dreams will be more telling." He pours a few droplets from both bottles onto a ceramic dish and then dabs his fingers into the mixture. He rubs the oils onto my forehead, behind my ears, and at both sides of my neck. It smells sweet, like flowers and syrup, like freshly picked fruit. His fingers are warm on my skin. They draw upward over my throat and then cup my chin. Jacob kisses me—a full, long kiss that turns my insides to a warm and sugary paste, like honey. "Sweet dreams," he whispers, getting up to leave.

"No," I say. "Stay. You'll help me fall asleep."

"Just what every guy wants to hear."

"You know what I mean." I get up from the bed and pull a suitcase from the back of my closet. The suitcase is full of all my spell supplies. I take out a stick of jasmine incense—coupled with the jasmine oil, it's sure to help me focus better in my dreams. I also take out a spool of yellow thread, a thin, plum-colored candle to help dispel confusion, a candleholder, and a jar of rainwater I've been saving.

I light the incense and set it down on its holder. The smoke rises up in puffy, grayish swirls. I breathe it in and close my eyes, mentally preparing myself for traveling in my dreams, trying to picture something that reminds me of sleep. I imagine the rain coming down outside my window, even though it's sunny out; I imagine it warm and runny on my skin, bathing me, preparing me for the most delicious sleep. I open my eyes and charge the rest of the ingredients by passing them three times through the incense smoke. Then I cut a long piece of thread from the spool and dunk it into the rainwater. "This water's been bathed in three full moon cycles," I tell Jacob. "I've been saving it for something important."

"Where did you learn this spell?" he asks.

"I got it out of there." I gesture to my family scrapbook, taking up a huge part of my suitcase. It's old and tattered and at least six inches thick. My grandmother gave me the scrapbook just before she passed away. It's basically this mishmash of stuff—spells, home remedies, bits of poetry, and favorite recipes—all written by people in my family before me, those like me who have the gift of insight.

I flip the book open and show Jacob the spell we're doing—a spell written by my great-great grandmother to unbind secrets. I'm thinking that since the voice in my dream—Clara's voice—told me not to tell anyone, that there must be some dark, obstructive secret underlying this whole thing.

I stir the piece of thread three times clockwise in the rainwater, concentrating on the color yellow for clarity, making sure it gets thoroughly submerged. Then I take it out and run my fingers down its length, a few droplets of water falling back into the jar. Meanwhile, Jacob charges the candle with the jasmine and lemongrass oils. His fingers fully saturated with both, he traces along the candle stem from north to south, west to east, and then he places the candle down in the holder on my night table.

"So now what?" he asks.

I take the thread and tie my first knot in it. "I need to tie as many knots as I have questions—as I want my dreams to answer."

"And what's the first question?"

"I want to know what Clara's secret is. And my second," I say, tying another knot, "is why I can't tell anyone." I tie a couple more knots, wondering how and if she'd really make me pay if I told anyone her secret. And then a couple knots more for the blood—for why my nose is bleeding and if it has anything to do with Clara's secret.

I wind the knotted thread around the plum-colored candle and then light the wick, extinguishing the wooden match with a snuffer so as not to confuse the energies in the room. "As clear as water and as loud as rain," I say, "may these secrets burn down as quick as a flame. For all that is hidden and all left untold, may you trust me enough to let these secrets unfold. Blessed be the way."

"Blessed be," Jacob repeats.

We snuggle up together on my bed, taking turns sipping the raspberry tea, eating a couple of the cookies, and watching the candle as it burns its way down through each knot.

eleven

It's dark, probably well past midnight, and I can't seem to stop shaking. I'm sitting alone on the beach, the chilling ocean air slicing right through me, sending shivers all over my skin. As each rain droplet hits against my body, it turns to ice and rolls off me, leaving a welt. In the distance, I can see the shadow of someone walking along the water. I squint to try and make out the figure. At first it looks like Clara. I can make out the sarong—a coral color, I think. It's wrapped tightly about her waist. The extra fabric flares out behind her in the wind. And I can almost make out her hair, the dark henna-red color just visible in the moonlight. I call out to her but she ignores me and continues walking farther and farther away.

I go to stand up, but I can't. I can't get my legs to work right. Icy water drips down my forehead and over my lips. It drains into my mouth and collects on my tongue.

"Don't tell anyone," whispers someone in my ear.

I turn to look, but I can't see anything. And it's dark all around me.

"If you tell, I'll know," she whispers. It's Clara's voice.

I look back out toward the water, but I don't see her anywhere. Instead I see the shadow of someone else—a guy, I think. The posture is stiffer, less languid, and it carries a certain darkness.

"If you tell, I'll make you pay." Her voice is coming from just above me now. I look up and a trickle of something drips down my face and onto my leg. I go to wipe it from my cheek. It's moist and dark between my fingers. Like blood.

"If you tell, I'll make you bleed," she whispers.

My heart throbs; tears stream down my face. The blood continues to trickle down the length of my thigh. I go to wipe it, noticing more blood running down my arm.

I look all around to find her, but there's only that other shadow, that guy, and he's coming right toward me. I scooch back in the sand to get away from him, still unable to stand. The rain has completely saturated the beach, making it hard to maneuver. Still, now on hands and knees, I work my way through it, closer to the cottage, away from him.

After managing a few yards, I turn and look back. He's still coming right toward me, a bouquet of some sort in his hands. Lilies, maybe.

The death flower.

I scramble forward as best I can, trying to get my legs to work right, but it's just no use. The rain continues to pelt my skin, turning the blood a slight pinkish color. I struggle to continue, the sand weighing me into the puddles now forming at my hands and feet.

"I'll make you bleed, Stacey," her voice continues. "You'll bleed until there's nothing left."

I try to stand again, almost able to get myself up. But after a couple steps, I feel my legs collapse and my world start to spin. I just feel so weak. So tired, like I'd give anything to sleep. I take two full breaths, noticing the tinkling of wind chimes in the distance.

"Just rest now, Stacey," she whispers. "Rest will make it all go away."

My cheek pressed flat against the rain-soaked sand, I force my eyes to open. He's still several yards away, but moving closer by the moment. I blink hard to try and focus on his face, but it's so blurry and dark, and my head won't stop spinning.

Using all the strength in my arms, I lift myself up, back on hands and knees, and make it up onto the back deck. I reach up for the door handle but end up falling backward, smacking hard against my shoulder and hip.

The wind chimes bong even louder, so piercing I almost want to cover my ears to block them out. I go to reach up for the knob again; this time I'm able to wrap my hand around it. I open the door, crawl inside, and lock the door behind me.

"Amber?" I call out. "Drea? Is anybody home?"

But there's only silence. I try standing again. My knees are wobbly and weak as I struggle to my feet. I flick on the light switch, the sudden blast nearly blinding me. But when I'm able to focus, it's like I don't know where I am. It's our cottage, but everything looks different—changed, like someone's rearranged all our things. I look to the coffee table. There's a knife sitting on it. I grab it for protection, noticing right away that it's really a letter opener—the old-fashioned kind with a curly handle and a pointed blade. I grip the handle and stumble to the front door to make sure it's locked, but before I can even get there, the door blows open and makes a knocking sound against the wall.

And then all the lights go out.

I take a deep breath and do my best not to cry out. He's here. Inside. I can feel it. Can feel him.

"Come on out," he whispers. "I don't bite."

The beating of my heart seems so loud, almost audible, like it could give me away at any second. I work my way slowly and quietly to a corner, away from the light of the windows, the moon casting in. Here, it's safe to look around. His figure moves in front of the bay window in the living room. It appears as though he just came out of Jacob's room. As though he's coming right toward me. I back up farther against the wall, but it's like I can't move—can't get away. Like I'm trapped in place.

"Stacey," he breathes. The wooden floor creaks with each step he makes toward me. "Can you hear me?"

Tears stream down my face. I hear myself whimper, my breath choking up inside my throat. I tighten my grip around the letter opener, readying myself to fight.

"Stacey . . . are you all right?" He tugs at my arm, jiggles me back and forth.

Until I wake up.

"Jacob," I say, all out of breath.

"Yeah," he says, still lying beside me in bed. "You were crying."

I look by the side of the bed at the candle stump. We didn't end up falling asleep until after the candle had burned down through the knots, until after Jacob had extinguished the flame with a snuffer. I shake my head, disappointed that I didn't sleep longer, that I don't remember any secrets being revealed.

"I'm sorry," he says, leaning over to kiss me. "Did I screw up a premonition? It's just that you were whimpering a lot. I got scared."

"It's okay," I say, noticing how his lips taste like the sea. "I probably would have done the same."

"So do you remember anything?"

I nod, remembering pretty much *everything*—the shadows at the shoreline, not being able to stand, the cold, the words, being chased, the lilies.

"Death," I whisper. "The death flower. I dreamt about it."

"What death flower?"

"My grandmother taught me that lilies mean death. The guy in my nightmare was holding a whole bouquet of them, just like in the premonitions I was having about Drea a couple years ago."

"What do you mean?"

"In the nightmares I was having about Drea, there was this faceless guy and he was carrying a bouquet of lilies. It turned out to be Donovan. Maybe the guy in my dream was supposed to be him." The thought of him sends a shiver down my spine. After everything that happened, Donovan was sent to a juvenile detention center until his twenty-first birthday, still three years away. When he told the jury that he was in love with Drea, that his stalking—as most dubbed it—was the result of his confusing their friendship for loveship à la temporary insanity, I think they felt bad for him. *So* bad that it almost didn't even matter that someone else got killed in his path—an accident, he called it. And everyone believed him.

"Yeah, but why?" Jacob says. "That doesn't make sense. He's locked up."

"As far as I know."

"Did you see the guy's face in your dream?"

"No."

"So maybe it was someone else."

I shake my head, getting more confused by the second. And then it occurs to me. I look at Jacob, at the murky aura that surrounds him. "Did *you* dream about anything?"

He looks away, obviously not wanting to tell me.

"Is that a yes?"

"I told you I can handle it."

"Are your nightmares the reason why you've been acting all quiet lately?"

"What are you talking about?" he asks. "I haven't been quiet."

"Last night at Cape Chowdah you barely said a word. And then when we came back to the house and played Pictionary with everyone, you were still kind of mute. Plus, yesterday morning when Clara came over . . . you sort of clammed up, and then when I looked back you were gone. It's like you haven't quite been yourself lately."

"I have a lot on my mind, Stacey." He sinks back into the pillow and chews his bottom lip, his aura all hazy and gray.

"I know, so we should talk about it. Is it that you don't trust *me*?"

"How can you ask that?" He reaches out to my forearm.

"Then what?"

"Then nothing."

"Fine." I clench my teeth. "Maybe I need some air."

"Stacey—wait."

I go to get up and a trickle of blood rolls down my lip.

Jacob grabs a wad of tissues and applies it to my nose.

"Thanks," I say, pulling back a bit.

"Don't be mad at me. I'm doing this for us."

For us? Is he serious? The idea that he expects me to believe that only infuriates me more. "Keeping secrets doesn't bring people together; it only pulls them apart."

"Is that really how you feel?"

I look at him, into his grayish-blue eyes, the color of steel—and yet they look like they could break at any second. "How do *you* feel?"

"I love you," he says.

I nod and look away, swallowing down the moment of awkwardness.

"Say something." He takes my hand, forcing me to look at him.

My chin shakes. Part of me wants to yell at him for keeping secrets from me. The other part wants to tell him how much I care. I slip into Amber's pair of frog slippers and press the wad of tissues firmly over my nose. "I'm gonna get a glass of water."

"That's it?" His voice rises.

But I don't know what else to say, and I don't want him to see me get teary over this. I stumble my way out the door and into the hallway, maneuvering the corners of the tissue to blot my eyes so I can see. But I almost can't believe *what* I'm seeing.

It's Clara. She's sitting on the living room sofa with PJ. He's consoling her—wiping her red and weepy eyes, cuddling her with an arm, and bringing a freezer-chilled glass of lemonade up to her lips.

"Stacey," she says, almost surprised to see me.

PJ lets out a sigh as though my sudden presence has infringed upon his attempts at seduction.

"Are you all right?" I ask her.

She shakes her head and wipes her runny eyes. "We really need to talk."

twelve

I ask Clara if she wants to take a walk somewhere so we can be alone to chat, but she declines. "Let's just talk here," she says. "I don't have anything to hide." She peers over at PJ, still sitting on the sofa, which perks him right up from slouch mode.

"What's going on?" Jacob emerges from my room, his hair all disheveled from our nap, his eyes a bit red.

"You remember Clara," I say.

He nods, taking a moment to glance at her, but then he focuses back on me, probably feeling as much as I do that we have some unfinished business to attend to.

But first I have some business with Clara.

While Jacob goes off to his room, Clara and I take a seat at the kitchen table.

"So," Clara begins, her lips all grimaced. "Something's going on."

PJ joins us at the table, his posture completely turned toward Clara like he's genuinely concerned, even though I know he's just trying to score himself a date. He plucks at his hair spikes, checking for proper alignment, maybe, and props his elbow on the table to listen.

"Someone was in my room," she says, her hands all fluttery from nerves.

"What do you mean?"

"I mean, after our conversation at the Clam Stripper, I went back to my cottage, went into my room to change, and noticed it right away."

"Noticed what?" PJ leans in farther, practically sitting in her lap now.

"My stuff was moved around."

"What stuff?" I ask.

"Random stuff—like my diary. I usually keep it under my bed, but instead it was just lying there on my corner chair. And my bathrobe. Normally I just drape it at the foot of my bed, you know, so I can just grab it easily, but someone hung it on the door hook."

PJ's shaking his head emphatically, like this is the worst turn of events he's ever heard, but all I can think is how it sounds pretty typical. How if it wasn't for my kicking skills, maneuvering through the gobs of laundry Amber, Drea, and I manage to deposit on the floor of our room, I probably wouldn't be able to find a thing.

"Is that it?" I ask, sensing the bitchiness of my words. "I mean, was anything else moved?"

"Oh yeah," she says. "My hairbrush. It was on the left side of my vanity table. Not the right."

"Maybe your mom came in and did some rearranging while you were out."

Clara shakes her head. "My parents are visiting some friends of theirs this week. It's just me."

"*All* alone?" PJ asks, horns sprouting up on his head. He gets up from the table to fetch a container of mayonnaise and a jar of sour pickles from the fridge. He opens both and sets them in front of Clara as an offering. "Comfort food, my little damsel-in-a-dress." He glances down to admire her sarong, or more accurately, the juicy thigh that peeks out through the slit. "Trust me," he says, "a few of these and the world will seem like a much happier place."

Clara cocks her head at him, like she doesn't quite get it. PJ responds by extracting a fat and bumpy pickle from the jar, dunking it into the mayo, and taking a big and crunchy bite. He closes his eyes in sheer delight, like it's the best thing since the plate of Mallomars Jacob fixed for me.

I'm just about to tell PJ that Clara and I could definitely use some alone time when I see her follow his lead. To my complete and utter shock, she takes out a big green mother of a pickle, dips the *entire* thing in the mayo, and crunches down.

"This is actually pretty good," she says, smiling for the first time since we've sat down. She double-dunks her pickle and takes another bite, making yummy-good groans the whole time. PJ follows suit—for him the ultimate test of love, I'm sure—sharing the mayo jar.

"We should really talk about your room," I say, forcing the look of horror off my face.

More groans.

"Um, Clara?" I repeat in an effort to interrupt the little food-love thing they've got going between them. Clara is looking up at PJ, her runny eyes a little bit calmer than just minutes ago. She smiles at him between crunches, a globule of mayo stuck to the corner of her mouth.

"Oh yeah," she says, as though forgetting I was even here. "Sorry."

"So was there anything missing?"

She shakes her head and grabs another pickle.

"Okay," I say, racking my brain for something else to ask. If it wasn't for my nightmares, for the cold vibrations that came over me when I touched her hand, I probably wouldn't even bother. I mean, if I didn't know better, I'd say she's completely just looking for attention.

"Was the door unlocked?" I persist. "Did you notice if any of the windows were left open?"

"Well, yeah, I always leave a few windows open to let the air in."

"The ones on the first floor?"

She nods. "There only *is* one floor."

"Right." I bite the inside of my cheek.

"I know it sounds all funky," she says. "But if you knew me, you'd know that I'm an extreme neat-freak."

"You, too?" PJ asks, accidentally dribbling pickle juice on the table. He attempts to wipe it up with his hand and then licks his fingers.

Clara eyes the dribble and continues to explain: "I have this thing about putting things in just the right spot. I'm one of those people who has a place for everything and puts everything in its place—notebooks, top left drawer of my desk; tissue box, top of my desk on the right; gum, in the ceramic seashell bowl on the dresser; white socks, at the front of my sock drawer; blue socks—"

"I keep an impressive stash of chewy things myself." PJ looks at her, taking a giant, purposeful bite of pickle. "Care to sample the inventory, my little kosher dill?"

I ignore PJ and keep focused on Clara, on how she's chewing on her thumb now. "You're really bothered by this."

She nods.

"And you're sure you didn't maybe just have a bad day and put stuff away in the wrong place?"

"No," she sighs. "You don't understand." She takes a deep breath to calm herself down. "My mother is blind. Her whole life is about order, about putting things in just the right spot. If she didn't, she'd never be able to find anything. So I've sort of become the same way."

"I'm sorry," I say. "I didn't know."

"How could you have? I mean, you're not psychic."

I pause at the comment, at the sheer irony of it, but choose not to respond. Sometimes I think my grandmother's secret to getting the answers was to keep her mouth shut—being comfortable with the silence, knowing how to listen to people, how to keep a firm bite on the tongue, and just let people babble the answers out for themselves.

"I'm really scared, Stacey. Especially after everything you said earlier."

"What did you say?" PJ turns to me.

"She said I was in trouble," Clara blurts. "She said something bad is going to happen to me."

Clara slumps into PJ's arms, and he mouths me an enthusiastic "thank you," like I plotted this whole thing for the sake of his lackluster love life.

The door whips open a second later. It's Amber. Her eyes lock on PJ and Clara. "What's going on?"

"It's what we were talking about earlier," I say. "About Clara."

But it seems Clara's welfare is the last thing on Amber's mind. Amber folds her arms in front, her jaw locking into stress mode.

"Is everything okay?" I ask her.

"Perfect," she says, eyeing PJ and Clara, clutched together as though for dear life.

"Hi, Amber," Clara says, resting her head on PJ's shoulder.

"Hi," Amber says, her face completely deadpan.

"Hey there, Miss Thing," PJ beams. He wipes the mayo-dribble from the corner of Clara's mouth and cuddles her against his chest. "Something bothering you?"

Amber shakes her head and retreats into our room, which *almost* surprises me. It's just that after all the time PJ has spent trying to win her back after their break up, not to mention all the boys she's dated in the meantime—probably more than there are pickles in the jar they're snacking from—I forget how territorial she can be with him.

"Is she okay?" Clara asks.

"Just perfect," PJ says, a huge grin married to his face.

"We need to focus," I say, grabbing at the sudden ache in my head. "Where were we?"

"Something bad's gonna happen to me." Clara huffs.

I rub my temples, trying to gain mindfulness, trying to concentrate despite the chaos going on all around me. Regardless of how bland her story might sound—a few random items misplaced in her room, especially while her mother is away visiting friends—Clara's life is truly in danger. I need to do my best to listen to her, to help her, and to stop the danger before it happens.

"You said that in your nightmare I was whispering something," Clara continues.

I nod, thinking about it a moment, about my nightmares and what I saw in them exactly. And then it hits me. In the nightmare I just had, when I struggled my way on hands and knees from the beach to the cottage, when I crawled inside the door and looked around, I saw that everything in the cottage had been moved around, rearranged.

Just like Clara was saying.

"Um, Mars to Stacey," PJ says, snapping his fingers to get my attention.

"Wait," I say, leaning forward to focus on Clara. "I need you to start over; tell me everything that happened again."

"Again?" She cocks her head.

I nod and she obliges, reiterating every detail about her journal, her bathrobe, and her hairbrush. "Oh," she lights up. "And my letter opener. Normally it's in my desk drawer, but instead it was on my night table."

My heart jumps, remembering how I saw a letter opener in my dream, how I was using it as a knife for protection. "Is your letter opener shiny silver with a curly handle and a knifelike blade?"

Clara's eyebrows furrow. "Yeah, how did you know?"

"Lucky guess." PJ snickers.

"What matters is that I believe you," I say. "I believe your stuff was moved around. And I believe that someone besides you moved it."

Clara's face falls and then her hands start to do that fluttering thing again. They tremble midair in front of her eyes, as though she's trying to cool herself off—or simply hold it all together. It's almost as if my believing her and acknowledging what happened has made it worse, like maybe she could have been talked into believing that she simply mislaid the stuff in her mother's absence.

"You told me something bad was going to happen," she says.

"Not with me around." PJ goes to crack his knuckles, but his fingers are as loud as he is helpful.

"So what now?" Clara asks. "Should I call the police or something?"

I shake my head. "There's no evidence. They'll just think you put your things back in the wrong place and label you temporarily insane."

"Yeah, but you can tell them about your nightmares, about how you dreamed about me."

"And then they'll label *me* temporarily insane."

"We need to be crafty," PJ says, rubbing his palms together.

"I need you to be super aware of where you put stuff for the next few days," I say. "If someone went through your stuff once, I'm sure they'll do it again. Until that time, keep your doors and your windows closed and locked."

"So I'm just supposed to sit around until someone breaks in and goes through my stuff again? What if I'm home when they do it? What if they want to hurt me?"

"I won't let them," I say, but even as I do I remember the blood in my dream and how I saw the death lilies. How there was some guy carrying a whole bouquet of them following after me.

thirteen

I tell Clara that she's welcome to stay at our place but she declines, even when I insist. PJ agrees to accompany her back, a bright and cheery smile across his sunblock-white lips.

"I think I should come, too," I say. "Maybe I'll be able to sense something."

"No," Clara says. "I mean, not right now. I'm not sure I could take it if you were able to sense something else."

"Then when?"

"Don't give it another thought, Stacey-bee." PJ drapes his arm around Clara, accidentally elbowing her ear in the process. "With me around, Clara will be as safe as a ten-dollar bill slipped down the front of a spinster's bustier."

"Do spinsters even wear bustiers?" Clara cocks her head in thought.

"Just ask Stacey," he says, winking at me.

"Maybe you could come over later," Clara says to me. "Right now, I think I'd just like to make sure everything is secure and in place."

"You should probably call your parents, too," I suggest. "Maybe they'll come back early."

Clara looks away, like maybe she's not so sure. Or maybe she doesn't want to tell her parents yet.

I see them to the door—PJ, with his arm draped around Clara's shoulders, and Clara, leaning into PJ just enough to show interest. The sight of them together like that reminds me that I should go and talk to Jacob. I turn toward his room, but then remember Amber coming in and how upset she seemed.

I knock on the door before going in. Amber is lying on her bed, staring up at the ceiling, the empty plate that formerly held the Mallomars sitting beside her, chocolate driblets at the corners of her mouth.

"Did you see them like that?" she gasps. "PJ and Miss Hula Girl . . ." She sits up in bed and folds her arms.

"I know," I say, plunking down beside her.

"I thought she was supposed to be after that Casey guy," she continues.

"Amber, I had no idea. I mean, maybe a little, but—"

"What?" Her cheeks puff up in anger. "About Casey?"

"No," I say. "I had no idea that you were still interested in PJ. I mean, I know you guys flirt, but after all this time of him trying to get you back—"

"Are you dizzy?" she snaps. "I'm *not* interested in him."

"Okay."

"It just totally bugs me out when I hear about some hula girl breaking up relationships and then coming over here and hanging all over a friend of mine. I mean, I don't have to be in freaking *love* with PJ to care about him. You of all people should understand that."

Instead of telling her that she's had ample opportunity with PJ—stomping on his heart every chance she gets— instead of pointing out that she doesn't even know Casey (never mind the details of what happened between him and his girlfriend), and instead of reminding her that I do indeed know a thing or two about caring for a friend— sometimes caring so much that I nearly get myself killed in the process—I take the dirty Mallomar plate for an emergency refill.

"Stacey—wait."

I turn around.

"Don't go. I'm just PMSing big time." She lets out a giant sigh. "I went next door, you know, to see if Sully wanted to go for a swim, and he totally dissed me. Can you believe that? He only asked me if I had my deposit money for the cruise Thursday night. By the way, are you going?"

"Not if I can help it."

"Well, then, can I borrow twenty bucks?"

I bite my tongue, taking an example from my grandmother's silence, thinking to myself how with a self-absorbed, PMSish attitude like that, it's no wonder she got dissed.

"Sully said he had some errands to do," she continues.

"So maybe he did."

"He had a freaking *bodyboard* in his hand, Stacey. What, am I not cute enough or something?"

"Of course you are."

"Then what?" she whines.

There's a knock on the door. Drea's standing there. "Can I get in on this conversation?"

"I don't want to hear it." Amber falls back on her bed.

"Trouble in paradise?" Drea asks.

"My love life doesn't have a paradise," Amber moans. "On second thought, my love life doesn't even have a life."

"Hold that thought," I say, remembering Jacob next door. I head to his room to try and salvage what's left of *my* paradise. I knock on the door but there's no response. "Jacob?" I eek the door open, but no one's even in there. Just boy-mess everywhere—pizza cartons stacked at the foot of PJ's bed, dirty laundry littered about the floor, and half-drunken Gatorades lined up on Chad's night table. Aside from the different taste in snacks—chocolate over pizza and Diet Cokes in place of Gatorades, their room is not unlike ours.

I go to Jacob's bed, noticing the dream box on his pillow. It's sort of like mine—smallish with chrome hinges, only instead of pine, his is made from a knotted hickory. I pick it up, wanting more than ever to know what he's dreaming about, wondering why he won't just tell me.

I close my eyes and do my best to concentrate on the box, feeling the knots of wood beneath my fingertips, hoping to gain the answer. But the only vibrations I feel in my fingers are the ones I got from Clara—that cold, tingling sensation.

"What are you doing in here?" Drea asks, completely startling me. The dream box tumbles from my grip.

"You scared me," I say.

She's standing in the doorway, arms folded like this is *her* room and not theirs. "Didn't mean to scare you," she says, "but what *are* you doing in here?"

"What does it look like?"

Amber peeks over Drea's shoulder and pushes past her into the room. "It looks like you're snooping through the guys' stuff without letting us in on the action. Let's see," she continues, looking around, "if I were a piece of something scandalous—"

"You already are," Drea interrupts.

"So true." Amber smiles at the unintended compliment. She moves over to Jacob's dresser and starts rummaging through the top drawer.

"I don't think so." I hop from the bed and jump in front of her, doing my best to keep her back.

"What's with the schoolmarm attitude? Afraid of finding something interesting?" Amber reaches around me and snags a pair of boxers from the drawer—gray with thin black stripes. "On second thought," she says, inspecting the merchandise, "looks like *his* stuff might be just as snoreful as yours."

"Not that it's any of your business," Drea adds.

"You just don't want me to start fishing through Chad's stuff."

"No," Drea says, folding her arms in front. "I don't." She stands behind Amber, helping me to box her in before she does any real damage.

"Fine, be that way," Amber squawks. "But don't come crying to me when you both find out that your seemingly picture-perfect significant others are really closet exotic dancers at the Shaky Snake."

"We're hardly talking about *your* ex-beaus," Drea says.

Amber ignores the comment and stuffs Jacob's boxers back into an already crammed drawer. She goes to close it back up but it's just too packed.

"Here," I say, grabbing the drawer handles, "let me do it."

Amber steps out of the way and I press both palms down on the heap of clothes. Still no go. I start rearranging his stuff, trying to get it as pancake-flat as possible, and that's when I spot it. His journal.

"Jackpot," Amber squeals.

"No," I say. "This is Jacob's; it's private."

"Are you freaking serious? Let 'er rip. Don't you want to know what he says about you?"

I press the journal between both palms, almost tempted to have a peek, to see what he's been hiding from me, what he's been dreaming about. I look at Drea, now busying herself by glancing over Chad's belongings.

"Did you even know he kept a journal?" Amber asks.

I want to tell her that I *did* know—that I know that he writes in it every morning upon waking up and that he sometimes reads me passages from it. But instead I opt for the truth and shake my head.

"See what I mean?" Amber says, tapping her teeth in thought. "A closet journal-keeper. Just when you think you know someone."

"Oh-so-scandalous," Drea mocks, her head buried in Chad's sock drawer. "Be serious. It doesn't mean anything. *I* keep a journal."

"Does Chad know about it?" I ask.

"Well, yeah, but so what?"

"So why didn't Jacob tell Stacey?" Amber asks.

"Listen," Drea says, "just because *your* love life is less than nonexistent these days doesn't mean you have to try and cause rifts in everybody else's. Stacey's a little more secure than that."

"Unlike you," Amber says, eyeing Drea on her fishing expedition.

"I'm not snooping," Drea says. "I'm just helping Chad reorganize."

"Well, then can we start reorganizing under the mattress?" Amber asks. "Because I'm thinking that's where the interesting stuff is going to be."

"I give up," I sigh, stuffing Jacob's journal back inside the drawer beneath a heap of T-shirts to avoid further temptation.

"Don't give it a second thought," Drea says to me. "All you need to do is bring up the subject of journals with him. Then I'm sure he'll tell you all about it. It probably just never came up."

"You're right," I say. But maybe the journal is a secret, too.

Drea reaches for something at the back of Chad's drawer and pulls out a box of some sort. Her face falls. She turns the box over, the front side facing Amber and me. There's a picture of some hairy-faced guy, his thumb and index finger doing that chin-scratch thing like he's in deep thought.

"What is it?" Amber asks.

But the answer is actually staring right at us in blue and gold lettering—"Nifty Over Fifty Moustache and Beard Darkener."

"Maybe it isn't his," Drea says.

"Right," Amber smirks. "I mean, just because it was in *his* drawer, with *his* stuff, on *his* side of the room . . ."

Drea opens the box and takes out the plastic applicator gloves. "I don't think Chad can even grow a beard."

"So maybe that's why he needs it," Amber says. "Maybe he plans to paint his face with it." She grabs the box, kisses the picture of Grizzly Adams on the cover, and then reads the color code in the corner: " 'Dark Bravado Blonde, Number 143.' The name alone makes my loins all aquiver."

"Okay," Drea says. "I think I've seen enough." She snatches the box back, stuffs the gloves inside, and crams everything back in the drawer.

Meanwhile, my head is spinning. I peer back over at the dream box on Jacob's bed and body-shove the dresser drawer closed. "Maybe we've *all* seen enough."

"Are you okay?" Amber asks.

Instead of answering, I just exit the room, slamming the door behind me maybe a little too hard. The noise practically rattles through the house. I go back into our room and make an effort to close the door behind me, but Drea intercepts.

"Stacey," she says, taking a seat beside me on the bed. "What is it?"

"I'm just feeling really stressed."

"Well, yeah, that part's pretty obvious. Is it about the journal?"

"It's about everything."

"Not *everything*," Amber interrupts. She comes and butts herself (quite literally) into the middle of our conversation, plopping down between us on the bed. "It's about the nightmares. I mean, *obviously*—waking up in a face full of blood is enough to stress anybody out. *That* and having to listen to a teary-eyed hula girl while she hangs all over PJ."

"What did I miss?" Drea asks.

"Clara," I say. "She was here earlier."

"Is it me," Drea asks, "or does anyone else think she's absolute bargain-basement material?"

"Because she called Chad cute?" I smile.

"Because she's an absolute skank," Amber clarifies.

"She says someone's been going through her stuff," I say.

"Do you believe her?" Drea asks me.

I nod and tell them everything—everything that Clara said about her misplaced items and her self-proclaimed neatness.

"So what now?" Drea asks.

"I had another nightmare about her."

"Did you actually *see* her this time?" Drea grabs a nail file from the top of her dresser.

"I saw her shadow—I know it was her. I heard her voice."

"So what did she say in the dream?" Drea takes my hand and begins filing away at my stubby nails. "What did she do?"

"She said more of the same—that I'm not supposed to tell, that if I do, she'll know and she'll make me pay."

"Anything else?" Amber tosses a bottle of nail polish to Drea.

I nod, noticing the neon-green color. "She said that if I tell, she'll make me bleed."

"Are you bleeding in the dream?" Drea asks.

"That's just it. I don't think I am. There's blood, but I think it's hers and that it's dripping on me. It's just weird, you know, to have someone's blood on me—on my hands— like I'm responsible if something bad happens."

"Don't think like that," Drea says.

"How can I not? I mean, I *will* be responsible. I'm the one who's having premonitions about her. I'm the one who's supposed to stop the danger."

"You do the best you can," Drea says. "You can't save the world."

"Easy for you to say now, seeing that Stacey saved your ass two years ago." Amber turns toward me. "But she's right, you know. You can't save the world—no matter how hard you try."

And I can't bring Maura and Veronica back. I glance down at my hands, picturing the imaginary stains of blood.

"Are you okay?" Drea asks.

"I will be."

"So obviously that's why your nose has been bleeding," Amber says. "Because of the blood in your dreams."

"I guess, but I don't know. That seems a little *too* obvious."

"All I know is that it's so freaking heinous," Amber says. "I mean, what do you do if you're making out and it slides down your throat and gets on your tongue and Jacob ends up with vampire-mouth?"

"Only you would think of that," Drea says, rolling her eyes.

"There's more." I swallow hard, trying to relax, to focus on the nail file as Drea attempts to square off my nail stubs. "Donovan was in my dream."

Drea stops filing to look up at me, her face completely frozen.

I nod. "At least I think it was him. I'm not sure. There was this guy coming toward me, and he was carrying a bouquet of lilies, just like in the nightmare I had about you."

"Death lilies," Drea says, covering her mouth.

"But you didn't see for sure that it was him," Amber says. "I mean, maybe it's just the lilies that you need to concentrate on. Maybe it was some other guy."

"Maybe," I say, looking back at Drea, at the plum-purple haze that surrounds her head. Maybe I shouldn't have said anything.

"Donovan still has another few years in juvie," Amber says.

"You're right," I say, nodding to reassure myself that he couldn't possibly have gotten out early.

"And, plus," she continues, "why would he ever come after Clara? That totally doesn't make sense. If anything, he'd come after Drea again. Or *you*."

"Is that supposed to be comforting?" Drea drops the nail file and buries her head in her hands.

"It'll be okay," I tell her, shooting a nasty look at Amber.

"Totally," Amber says, completely oblivious. She plucks the nail file from the bed and files away at her thumbnail.

"It's not Donovan we need to focus on right now. It's death."

Right, I think to myself. *Death.* As though the revelation in itself is supposed to be a good thing.

fourteen

Amber and Drea agree to help me do a de-stressing spell. I'm just so completely frazzled lately that I can't quite get a handle on things. I mean, yes, it goes without saying that the fact that Clara's life is on the line has got me a bit on edge. But I feel like there's something more. Something that's been causing my palms to get all sweaty, my chest to tighten up with each breath, and my head to feel all spinny, like I need to sit down. Maybe it's Jacob. Maybe it's because there's been this block in our relationship—he won't completely open up, and I can't completely tell him how I feel.

Or maybe it's just pure anger. I wanted this to be a normal summer—one last opportunity for all of us to be together before separating and going off to college. Instead I'm helping strangers. I tame my bitter mood with a fingerful of maple syrup, reminding myself that if it wasn't for people helping strangers—for Jacob helping me last year—I might not even be here right now.

"Stacey," Amber says, cracking a couple eggs into a ceramic bowl. "You look all fishy. Like you just swallowed a slimy one packed in oil."

We're standing around the kitchen island, whipping up a hefty serving of French toast, which in my opinion is the world's most perfect food—sugar mixed with thick, syrup-sopping, buttery bread.

"Well, she does have a lot on her plate right now." Drea pours a tablespoon of vanilla extract into the bowl.

"No pun intended," Amber says, holding up a plateful of dunking bread—big fat slices from a bakery-bought loaf.

"So lame," Drea says in response.

"I agree." I sprinkle cinnamon into the bowl and top everything off with a cup of milk and a couple teaspoons of apple juice.

"Since when is French toast a spell?" Amber asks.

"Since we're making it with the most important ingredient." I stir the batter up, concentrating on the apple juice as it blends with the other ingredients, on the apple fruit's ability to cleanse and heal.

"We're spiking the batter?" Amber perks up.

"No," I say. "We're making it together—as friends."

"Um, yeah," Amber says, cutting a couple butter blocks from the stick and dropping them onto the hot skillet. "Are you sure you don't want me to add in a little schnapps?"

"I'm serious," I say, dunking a piece of bread into the milky batter. "I'm feeling really alone right now, and I'm kind of counting on your friendship."

"Well, of course you have it," Drea says. "Whatever we can do to help."

"Just have some of this with me," I say, setting a sopping chunk of bread onto the bubbling griddle. "My grandmother used to say that there's something truly intimate about sharing food with the people you love."

"Intimate? Sharing food? People you love?" Amber raises an eyebrow. "Um, no offense, Stace, but it sounds like Gram was into food kink."

"Hopeless," Drea sighs.

I giggle my agreement.

We spend the next fifteen minutes or so taking turns dipping the bread, stirring the batter, and flipping the toast until we have a hefty helping of sheer deliciousness sitting high atop a plate. It's just what I need, actually—being with them and talking about normal stuff, like Drea's tan-line dilemma and tonight's episode of *The O.C.*

When none of us can bear to cram another piece of French toast into our bellies, I place a fully charged, moonbathed jar on the table in the center of us. "Here's where the de-stressing part comes in," I say.

"Let's hear it for Miss Recycle," Amber says, probably noticing that it's an old Smuckers jar I spared from the trash.

I place a box of paperclips on the table, as well as a dried and bound bunch of sage. The sage leaves are twiglike, all brittle and gray. I've wound them with thread for a cleaner burn.

"What's with the paperclips?" Amber asks.

"We're going to use them to represent things in our lives that bind us up in a negative way. Labeling these negative binds will help free us from stress."

"Maybe we should have stopped at Staples," Amber says, frowning at the shallow box of clips. "With the day I've had, I'm thinking I could label a whole crateful."

I unscrew the lid off the jar and set a box of wooden matches down beside it. I light the end of the sage and blow out the flame. It smokes up like incense; long and curly tendrils of smoke make their way toward the ceiling. I walk around the kitchen with the sage, smudging the room with its sweet and spicy scent. "The sage will help rid us of these negative binds."

"Yeah, but will it help rid us of the kagillion calories we just ingested?" Drea pats her belly.

"I'll start." I set the sage down on a ceramic dish in the center of the table and take one of the paperclips. "This clip represents the stress I feel about helping Clara." I drop the clip into the jar.

"I'll second the Clara stress." Amber takes a clip and drops it into the jar.

"Why is she stressing *you* out?" Drea asks.

"Because she's getting all flirty with PJ and maybe he can't afford to have his heart broken."

"Who says she's going to break it?"

"Oh, please," Amber says. "I know her type—the kind who flirts with anything in pants with no intention of anything serious."

"Oh, you mean girls like you?" Drea asks. "Is somebody jealous?"

"Hardly. Just don't be surprised when Little Miss Hula Girl starts getting all friendly with Chad." Amber drops another paperclip into the jar. "This is for Sully and how he doesn't know what he's missing."

Drea takes a paperclip and tosses it in. "This is for Chad, for the argument we had earlier."

"What was that about?" Amber asks.

Drea shrugs. "It was actually something about Stacey."

"It was?" I grab another paperclip.

"It was nothing really. He was just remembering something about you, and it kind of bothered me."

"What was it?"

"It's stupid, really." Drea rolls her eyes toward the ceiling, the way she always does when she doesn't want anyone to see what she's feeling. "I was telling him about this jealousy article I read in *Seventeen,* and I guess it was the way I was describing it—my voice kind of squeaking on a couple of the words, or so he said. Personally, I don't think my voice squeaks at all, but maybe I was super-into telling him or something. So anyway, he was staring at me really weird, and so I asked him what was up, and he said that my voice got all squeaky and that reminded him of you—you know, when you get nervous and your voice does that high-pitched thing? And then he just sort of sat there with this giant grin on his face, saying how cute it is—the squeaking, I mean. *Your* squeaking."

"Oh," I say. "But my voice *doesn't* squeak."

"Well, neither does *mine.*"

"Riveting," Amber says, poking the point of a paperclip through one of the holes in her Swiss-cheese earrings. She plucks another clip from the box and drops it into the jar. "Keeping with the whole love-sucks-worse-than-leeches theme, this clip is for Casey and how he didn't even look at me today."

"I'll tail that with the stress I've kind of been feeling with Jacob." I drop a clip into the jar.

"You two?" Amber balks. "Puh-leeze, all you two need is a little Clara-less time to yourselves. Why not be super-romantic and get a room to yourselves on the frat-boy cruise everybody's talking about?"

"Actually, I think *you're* the only one who's talking about it," I say.

"No," Drea says, straightening out one of the paper clips. "Chad was telling me about it earlier. It might be kind of fun."

"Well, you'll have to let me know," I say, "because I'm not going."

"Then how do you plan to patch up your problems in paradise?" Amber asks.

"Maybe they just need a small patch." I grimace. "Like lobster rolls and a walk on the beach."

"Sounds thrilling." Amber yawns.

We spend another twenty or so minutes adding in all the things that stress us, including bathing suits, tan lines, and sandy fried clams. Then I drop the sage into the jar and screw on the lid, the insides smoking up, painting the glass a grayish frosty color. "May these negative binds please leave our minds and be replaced by love and grace. O sage, I ask thee to oust our stress, and return to us all happiness. Blessed be."

"Blessed be," Drea says.

"Blessed be," Amber repeats.

fifteen

Several minutes after our spell, Jacob walks in. "Hi," he says, eyeing the smoke-filled jar.

"Hi." I stand up.

Amber and Drea instinctively get up from the table to leave us alone. "Homework project," Amber says, lamely trying to lighten the mood.

"Can I talk to you?" I ask him. Instead of waiting for his answer, I just go to him. I wrap my arms around his waist and snuggle my chin into the crook of his neck.

"I take it you're not still mad at me," he says.

"No," I say, "I am."

"Well, then, maybe I should screw up more often."

"Very funny." I say, noticing how he smells like citrus. "Let's go out."

"Out?"

I nod. "Like, on a date. Like normal."

"I could go for some normal." He squeezes me extra tight. "What did you have in mind?"

"Nothing fancy. How about a picnic on the beach? It shouldn't be as crowded at this hour. People have probably gone home for dinner."

"Sounds perfect."

Even though I can't even think about squeezing in another morsel, we fill a basket with crackers, cheese, and fresh fruit, and pick a spot close to the ocean. We talk for well over an hour, watching the sun as it pinkens and falls just above us. It feels good to be normal like this, to chatter on about stuff that makes us happy—how the theater downtown is having a Hitchcock marathon this weekend and maybe we should go, how relieved we are to be going to the same school in September, and how soothing it is to fall asleep to the sound of the ocean pulling at the sand.

I lay my head back against his chest and close my eyes, breathing in the lingering scent of coconut oil and relishing every moment. But, despite how good this feels, I still want to—*need* to—ask him about earlier. "Where did you go when Clara came over?"

"Just out for a walk."

"I didn't see you leave."

"I went out the front. I didn't want to interrupt you two." He brings my fingers up to his mouth, brushing them against his lips. "How did it go with her?"

I shrug. "She says that someone went through her stuff. But I don't know, I feel like there's so much *more* than that."

"Well, of course there's more," he says. "You sensed more when you shook her hand; you sensed more in your nightmares. It's only a matter of time before something major happens."

"Not if I have something to say about it."

"So you're feeling confident?"

"About Clara? I think so."

"And about everything else?"

I pause, trying to think of a nonchalant way to bring it up, some way that doesn't make me look like a big fat snoop. But since it's so completely obvious that I *was* indeed snooping, I spare him the insult to his intelligence, peek up into his face, and just say it: "I saw your dream box."

Jacob nods, his face all poker-playerish, like he isn't surprised at all.

"I mean, I saw it *out*. On your bed," I continue.

Jacob straightens up, forcing me to scooch up. "What were you doing in my room?"

"I was looking for you and there it was, just lying on your bed."

"I was out for a walk," he repeats.

"I know," I say, hearing that stupid nervous squeak in my voice. "You mentioned that already."

He nods, like he knows, too—like he's purposely avoiding the question.

"So are you going to tell me, or do I have to beg for it?"

"I'm doing this for *you,* Stacey."

"How is keeping stuff from me helping me?"

"You're going to have to trust me on this."

I clench my teeth, knowing that I do have to trust him, but also knowing that this isn't exactly fair. "I was hoping that maybe you had the dream box out because you wanted to help me, maybe tap into my nightmares somehow, so we'd be dreaming about the same thing."

"I *would* like that," he says.

I feel my face crinkle up at his response, like it's the first time the idea has occurred to him, when I was thinking all along that maybe that was the answer—that he had already started to dream about Clara, that he saw something in her fate that he didn't think I could handle.

So now what?

I want to ask him about the journal as well, but I almost feel as though that would win me the "insecure girl-friend/snoop of the year" award—second only to Drea, of course. Plus, before I can even get the words out, he kisses my hand and then leans in and kisses my mouth, sending a million tiny tingles down the length of my spine. "I'm proud of you," he whispers. "For being brave."

The compliment completely takes me aback. I mean, I've just never thought of myself like that before. I smile and weave my fingers through his, still tasting him in my mouth—like maple syrup mixed in vanilla fudge on my tongue. "You mean that?"

He nods, his slate-blue eyes focused on mine, like he really means it. Like I *am* brave, despite any tension I'm feeling about him or Clara or anything else.

We kiss some more, continuing to feel each other's hands—our palms when they touch and the heat of each other's skin. The moment is hypnotic, so amazingly good that I almost feel as though I could get completely drunk on it—on him—losing any of the reservations I've been having about our relationship or about trust. I mean, he's obviously doing what he feels is best.

Of course, that's when PJ interrupts us, ripping a wide-open gash in our long-awaited time alone.

"Hey kids," he sings.

Clara's standing a few yards behind him, an overnight bag slung over her shoulder.

"Did we interrupt anything Polaroid-worthy?" PJ asks.

"Hey guys," I say.

"Hay is for horses, my little mammal. We need to talk."

"What's wrong?" I sit up more.

"It happened again," Clara says. She drops her bag to the sand and comes and joins us.

"What did?" Jacob asks.

Clara pauses to smile at him, but she doesn't answer.

"Well?" I ask, in an effort to stop her from openly gawking at my boyfriend.

"Are your roommates around?" she says, finally. "I think they should hear what I have to say as well."

I shake my head, mentioning that Chad was out last I checked, wondering why she can't just spill it about what's going on—why she needs an audience. Still, I clean up the remainder of our picnic, and we go back inside the cottage to find Drea and Amber.

They're in our room. Drea is applying some creamy orange stuff to Amber's face—only Amber's eyes, nostrils, and lips are visible.

"In less than ten tiny minutes," Drea explains to me, "Amber will have skin as soft as a baby's butt. It's all natural; you can practically eat the stuff."

"I'll pass," I say.

"Your loss." Drea looks up from the jar to eye my skin, probably noting the blotchiness—a blending of paleness and sunburn.

"Clara wants to talk to us," I say, ignoring the thorough inspection.

"What for?" Amber scowls through the orange mask.

I shrug and wait for them to follow me out, Amber with her arms folded and her lips tightened into a frown. We all take a seat at the kitchen table.

"So what's with all the drama?" Amber asks.

"*You're* asking *us* about drama?" PJ says. "What's with the ghoulish goo on your face?"

"It's a mud mask," she corrects.

"Are you sure you used mud and not pig snot?"

"*You're* one to talk, with those white-ass lips. It looks like you were sucking face with Ronald McDonald," Amber retorts.

"It's called sunblock," PJ explains. "SPF 65—"

"In case you haven't noticed, the sun doesn't exactly *blaze* past 5 PM."

"I'm sorry to bother you guys," Clara says, interrupting them. "It's just—"

But she can't continue. She takes a couple big breaths to calm herself, but she's completely distraught—her eyes watering up, her hands doing that weird fluttering thing in front of her eyes.

"Allow *me,* my little damsel." PJ kisses the crown of her head, a few strands of her hair sticking to his sunblocked lips. "Picture it," he says. "Exterior—day. Sunny; beach setting; hoards of people, sunning and funning it up in the background. Two exceptionally good-looking beach babes, a boy and a girl, trot their way down a long beach strip seasoned with summer cottages."

"Time out," Amber says, waving a hand in the air. "Who are the exceptionally good-looking beach babes in this scenario?"

PJ's mouth snarls open. "If you aren't going to play nice, my thorny little bush, I think you should return to the dirty playground that you crawled from."

"Okay," I say in an effort to speed things up. "Obviously the good-looking people are Clara and PJ."

"Well, at least we have one bright little match who drank her carrot juice today." PJ shines me an approving smile, and I have to choke back my frustration. That or he'll be telling this story until well after midnight.

Jacob glances at his watch. "So what happened?"

"Happened?" PJ starts up again. "We were walking down the strip, minding our own biz-wiz, when we see this completely outlandish tentacle-man who dares to ask Clara-bear here if she can pose for some photo thing tomorrow afternoon."

"Wait," Drea says. "Why are we calling him a tentacle-man?"

PJ rolls his eyes in frustration. "Um, because he had *tentacles.*"

"*Seriously?*" Drea glances at Jacob and holds back her laugh.

"Not tentacles," Clara says. "Just an obnoxious mustache with rolled ends."

"Wait," I say, "is this that guy who lives next door, the one with the giant back porch?"

"Yeah," she says. "You know him?"

"Well, I kind of met him," I say. "Earlier, when I was looking for you."

Clara seems somewhat surprised; she cocks her head for just a second before continuing: "The guy seems, like, a total creepy creep. I've seen him on his back porch, taking pictures of girls on the beach—without them knowing. And I overheard some girl at the Clam Stripper saying how he's supposedly some brilliant photographer who does all this big-time freelance work for magazines like *Vogue* and *Esquire,* but I don't know. I mean, the guy is way weird. This isn't the first time he's asked to take my picture."

I nod, wondering if I should pay another visit to his cottage when he isn't home, cringing at the thought of that decrepit darkroom and the way he looked at me—how he wanted to take my picture. "So what did you say when he asked you to pose?"

"Well, of course I said no—yet again—but that still didn't stop him from looking at me like the creepy-creepy that he is. After that, me and PJ went to my cottage."

"The door wasn't even locked," PJ says, tisk-tisking Clara with his finger. "Anyone could have just slithered in there."

"Why wasn't it locked?" I ask.

Clara shrugs. "It's a pain carrying around a key, especially with a bathing suit."

I nod at her lack of common sense, noting how she's also wearing a sweatshirt with two perfectly good pockets. That and another sarong—a red one with bright gold flowers. "Which cottage is yours, anyway?"

"Number 24. The one with the bamboo wind chimes. I'm sure you've heard them. They're *so* obnoxious, but my dad really likes them."

I nod, wondering if those are the wind chimes I heard in my nightmare.

"Can we please get through this story, like, today?" Amber groans. "My face feels like it's fizzling." She grabs a paper plate and uses it as a fan.

"So anyway," Clara continues, "we went into my room and—" She's welling up all over again. "Someone went through my drawers."

"How do you know?" Jacob asks.

"Because they were open."

"At least one of them was." PJ snickers.

"Which one?" I lean in toward Clara and take one of her fluttering hands, the cold, biting sensation returning to my own hand, running up my arm and wrapping around the back of my neck.

"My underwear drawer." She blushes.

"*What?*" Drea gasps.

"Did they find anything interesting?" Amber plucks a tissue from the front of her bathing suit and hands it to a sniffling Clara.

"I don't know *what* they found." Clara pauses a moment to grimace at the tissue offering. "But they went through my things."

"How can you be sure?" Jacob asks.

"The telltale sign," PJ says. "Lace trim hanging out the sides. Straps thrown askew. Undies left in a tizzy. Like the skivvies themselves decided to party it up while the mistress was out. You know the saying, while the kitty's away . . ."

"You're so freaking weird." Amber balls up her tissue and throws it at him.

"For later, O queen of kink." PJ sniffs the tissue ball and then stuffs it into his pocket.

"So what you're saying is that you got panty raided?" I hand Clara a napkin, and she gratefully takes it.

"And you're sure you didn't just get ready extra fast this morning and leave your stuff like that?" Drea says.

"That's what the cops asked me."

"You called the police?" I feel my eyes widen.

Clara nods. "They even came over. But they weren't really surprised or mad about it or anything."

"Because the doors and windows weren't locked," PJ clarifies.

"They made a report and said that it was probably some boys playing a prank."

"Or maybe a fraternity pledge stunt," Drea says.

"The police suggested that, too."

"*Hel-looooo,*" Amber says, snapping her fingers. "Who pledges a fraternity in the summer?"

"So the police are gonna check it out," Clara says. "You know, go and talk to the frat boys who live next door."

"I'm telling you," Amber says, "it's not them. Casey and Sully are way too sweet and sensitive for stuff like that."

I look at Amber, completely funkified by her logic. I mean, *sweet* and *sensitive?* Am I totally missing something here?

"There are probably a lot of guys living in those frat houses," Drea says. "I saw a couple of them watching me on the beach earlier."

"I know." Clara shudders. "Some of them are so gross. They just openly gawk at . . . *anybody.*"

Amber gasps in response while Drea's mouth drops open in sheer loathing.

"Anyway," I say, wrapping an arm around Drea, literally holding her back from bopping Clara on the head. "Clara, you're obviously going to stay with us tonight."

"If it's okay," Clara says, blotting her eyes and nose with the napkin. "I called my parents. They were willing to drive back tonight, but it's like four-and-a-half hours from their friends' place, and it's already kind of late. They're coming back tomorrow, though; they're leaving first thing."

"Of course," I say, nodding. "We insist you stay here."

"That's what I told her you guys would say." PJ drapes his arm around Clara, smooshing her against his chest.

"Great," Amber says, dabbing at her mask of mud and bringing a fingerful up to her lips for a taste. "Just freakin' dandy."

sixteen

Before bed, we offer to shuffle up our sleeping arrangements to make Clara more comfortable. When PJ's attempt
to coerce Clara into his bed doesn't work, I offer to sleep
out on the couch while Clara takes my place. Except
Amber refuses to sleep in the same room with someone she
doesn't know—a first for her—and Jacob isn't comfortable
offering up his bed (probably because he has stuff to hide,
like journals and dream boxes). Top that off with Drea's

loathing for Clara, PJ's bed being too stinky for anyone else but him, Chad not really caring *where* he sleeps, but Clara completely weirded out at the idea of sleeping in the same room with guys. The end result is Clara sleeping out on the living room sofa, alone.

Before settling myself down to snooze, I punch my pillow a couple times for the optimum level of fluffage and glance over at the de-stressing jar on my bedside table. It's actually helping me quite a bit. I feel much calmer than I did earlier, almost restored, which is why the whole sleeping arrangement chaos doesn't drive me to grab my pillow and camp out on the sand—probably something I would have resorted to under normal circumstances.

I close my eyes, thankful that Jacob and I managed to work some things out, and then I do my best to focus on Clara. But, once again, I can't sleep. I just keep playing it over and over again in my mind—my dream, her voice, the blood, the idea of someone going through her stuff. But no matter how many times I go over it, there's just not enough to point me even remotely close to an answer. I need to have another nightmare; I need to bleed again, to figure out *what* exactly my body is trying to tell me.

I reach for the de-stressing jar, focusing on the sage inside, how the tip has completely blackened over. That's when I feel myself start to nod off.

It's also when I hear Clara calling me. I sit up in bed and look over at Amber and Drea to see if they can hear Clara calling me, as well. But they're still sleeping, completely unaffected by her voice.

I slide into my slippers and make my way out to the living room to see what she wants. But she isn't even out here. The sofa is all made up for sleeping—bed pillows piled high at one end and a blanket draped across length-wise—but no Clara.

"Stacey," she calls. "I need you."

Her voice is coming from the bathroom. I turn to look; the door to the bathroom is shut, but I can see from the door crack that the light is on.

"Clara?" I rap lightly at the door.

No response.

"Clara?" I knock a little louder.

Still nothing.

I press my ear up against the door. The faucet is running, so maybe she can't hear me. Maybe she's washing her hair in the sink. I try calling her a couple more times and knock even louder, but nothing seems to work.

I wrap my hand around the doorknob and turn it. "Clara?" I say, peeking in.

The faucet is on, steaming water pouring out into the sink, but she's not in here. I check the shower stall—empty.

"Stacey," she calls again. Her voice is coming from the kitchen now.

I shut off the faucet and move toward her voice. But she's not in the kitchen either, nor is she in the living room, our room, or the guys' room. And yet I can still hear her calling out to me. I move out onto the back porch. It's freezing out here. My ears sting from the chill. Goose-bumps sprout up on my skin.

"Stacey," she calls. "I need your help." It's almost as if her voice is part of the wind, howling in my ears.

I look out toward the water, but it's dark, the only light coming from the last quarter moon. It paints its reflection across the ocean's surface. I move out onto the sand, continuing to follow her voice, but it seems the closer I get to it, the farther away she moves. Her voice is just a whisper now—much weaker than before.

"Clara?" I call again. There are shadows following behind me. I keep looking over my shoulder to see who's there. But I can't see much farther than a few yards away.

The ocean tide is coming in fast, just an arm's length from my feet. Maybe Clara went for a swim. Or worse—maybe she couldn't sleep, went out on the beach for some air, and dozed off in the sand. I feel myself moving faster, almost running now down the length of the beach, using the waning moon as my light. Wind chimes play in the distance. I listen hard for their pitch—to see if they're the bamboo kind, a little bit deeper than the normal tinkling of bells and metal, but I just can't tell. Every time I try to concentrate on the sound, it seems Clara's voice plays over it. She's whimpering my name now, like maybe she's hurt.

I look up toward the strip of cottages and, for just a second, I think I see someone watching me from a window. I stop and squint, but it's too dark to be sure. I only know that I feel like I'm being watched. That someone's following behind me.

I walk for several more minutes, farther and farther down the beach. There's a street lamp up ahead. It blinks a couple times, casting its light over the cliff side—a jetty of rocks that leads from the ocean up toward the street. I stop a moment, focusing on the figure in the light. It's still several cottage-lengths away, but I can see someone there. The person is standing on a rock slab, and he's holding a bouquet. I know they're lilies. I can feel it, can feel death. It's like it's all around me.

My skin turns colder. My fingers numb up. I close my eyes and imagine the sun, its warmth. I wiggle my fingers, checking that I still have the power to move. I do. I open my eyes. The person holding the bouquet is now gone. But instead, lying in the sand, just a few yards away, is a long and narrow mound of some sort. That's when I know.

It's Clara. Her back faces me, but I recognize the coral-colored sarong. I move closer and see a long line of blood running down her thigh. I go to turn her over, to see where she's wounded, but I just find more blood—down her arms and on her belly. And now it's on me, like I'm already too late.

"Clara?" I call, shaking her a bit, feeling my insides tremble. I position her body closer to me, readying myself to give CPR. That's when I notice the bottle sticking out from under her arm. It's my old perfume bottle, the one I used for the spell I did at the beach, when I wrote DON'T TELL ANYONE onto a slip of paper, poked the paper into the bottle's mouth, and then threw it out to sea. I pick the bottle up, noticing my note still inside. I remove the cap and the paper slips out just as easily as it went in. I unroll it, my fingers shaking, trying to work right. I read the words, feeling my face funk up in confusion—I'LL MAKE YOU PAY. I double-check the bottle, making sure it's mine. It is.

Clara's body flinches a bit, as though from the cold. I call her name out a bunch of times and tap at her face, the way they do on TV to check if someone is conscious. But it doesn't seem like she is. Her body is limp. Her skin is pale. I place my ear at her mouth, to see if I can feel her breath against my cheek. But I don't. I go to check the pulse from her wrist, but that's when I feel myself pulled back, when I'm shaken out of sleep.

The light clicks on in our room, making me squint. It appears as though Drea has woken me up. She's sitting right beside me in bed, her hand resting on my shoulder. Amber plops down on the other side of me, her face completely covered in greenish aloe goop to replace the orange facial mask from before.

"You were breathing all weird," Drea says. "And convulsing, sort of. Your chest started doing this jumping-heaving thing."

"And not in a good way," Amber adds.

"Plus," Drea continues, "you were calling Clara's name out and that started giving *me* nightmares."

"Really?" I say, taking a big breath.

"You don't remember?" Drea asks.

"No," I say, rubbing my temples. "I guess I do remember. I just didn't realize I was moving around." I glance at the clock; it's 2:05 AM. "Where *is* Clara?"

"Sofa City, where she belongs," Drea says.

"No," I say, sitting up in bed. A trickle of blood rolls down my lip. I go to stop it with my fingers, getting blood all over the front of my hand, just like in my dream, like this is Clara's blood and I'm already too late.

"Heinous!" Amber screeches. She removes her frog slipper and throws it at me.

"How's that supposed to help?" Drea asks, handing me a value pack of tissues.

I grab the tissues and hop out of bed, practically trampling over Amber in the process.

"Wait," Drea calls out to me. "Where are you going?"

I whip open the door of our room and rush into the living room. Just as I dreamt, Clara isn't there.

seventeen

Without a second thought, I dash out of the cottage and run down the beach strip, sure I'm going to find Clara, remembering how she was calling out to me in my nightmare—like she really needed my help.

I scurry through the sand, keeping an eye on the water, using the moon as my light.

But I don't see her anywhere.

I'm thinking that maybe she went back to her cottage. Maybe she forgot something important—a contact lens case, some prescription medicine she might be taking, a favorite teddy bear . . . I remember her saying that her cottage is number 24 on the strip, that there's a set of obnoxious wind chimes on her back porch. But it seems like the sound of wind chimes is everywhere around me—deep baritone ones, subtle tinkling ones, and every kind of ping in between.

A wad of tissues still pressed against my nose, I move toward cottage number 24. The porch light is on and, just as Clara said, there's a huge set of bamboo wind chimes hanging at the top of the stairs. I stop a second to catch my breath and check my nose. It seems like the bleeding has stopped. I stuff the soiled tissues into the pocket of my pajamas and gaze up at the place. Despite the deck light being on, it doesn't appear as though anyone is inside. It's completely dark.

I climb the steps anyway, feeling suddenly as though I'm being watched, as though someone might even be following behind me. I peek over my shoulder and see a couple of shadows cross on the beach. Or maybe it's just my imagination. It's dark, the only light coming from the moon and the few cottages that have their deck lights on.

Just imagining someone inside her cottage, that cold, biting chill crawls up my arm and down my spine. I take a deep breath, remembering how in my nightmare I thought I saw someone watching me from one of the cottage windows. I look toward the window of Clara's cottage, wondering if this was the place. Or maybe it was at that photographer guy's place. I look next door, but it's too hard to tell. It's too dark and all the cottages look the same.

I swallow my fear in a deep breath and take a step closer to the door, remembering the feeling of death in my nightmare. It's like it's still with me, almost numbing me in place. I hold the amulet around my neck, reminding myself of strength. At least Clara's parents aren't home; I can freely ring the doorbell without having to worry about waking them up. I ring it a couple times, continuing to look over my shoulder for anyone who might be following, continuing to look toward the beach for Clara—for her body. Or for the person holding the bouquet of lilies.

Several moments pass, but still no one has come to the door. I try the knob and, to my surprise, it turns. I clench my teeth, remembering how we all spoke to Clara about locking things up, remembering how she and PJ came back here earlier to make sure everything was secured.

I edge the door open. "Hello? Clara?" I wait a couple seconds, my heart strumming hard, rattling me up completely. But no one responds. I push the door open wider and stick my arm in, feeling along the wall for a light switch. I find one and flick it on.

Just as Clara said, everything has a place—remote controls lined up on the coffee table, a collection of ceramic dolphins on the mantel arranged in a perfect ring, pillows set up on the couch according to size and color, drink coasters on the right of the end table, a stack of napkins to the left.

I move down the hallway toward the bedrooms. "Hello?" I call, my heart thumping even harder now. All the doors are closed. I go to open the one on the left. I feel along the wall for a light switch, but I can't seem to find one. I move in a little farther, opening the door completely to gain a bit of light from the living room. I can see there's a lamp by the bed. I click it on, my eyes taking a moment to adjust. And when they do, I can see this is Clara's room. The bed is covered in a bright purple comforter with peach-colored pillows, and there are a couple stuffed bears and a Discman on the night table.

I take a step farther inside, nearly choking on my breath. On the wall, right in front of me, are the words from my nightmare: I'LL MAKE YOU PAY.

My jaw shakes. My heart plummets. My skin turns cold—like ice. The words are written in a dark red color—like blood.

I clench my teeth to stop the quivering and, at the same moment, hear something out in the living room—the sound of the back door opening and then closing. I back myself up against the wall, behind the door, the words still staring at me. For just a second, I think about clicking off the light, but I know whoever is here would definitely notice.

The wooden floor creaks in this direction. It's only a matter of moments. I grab a ceramic vase from the bedside table, readying myself to fight. The footsteps get closer. It sounds as though there's more than one person. The door to Clara's bedroom creaks open. I clench the vase, bringing it high above my head.

"Hello?" calls a voice.

Drea?

She takes a couple steps into the room, her back toward me.

"What are you doing here?" I gasp.

Drea jumps, noticing me behind her.

"No," Amber says, pushing her way past Drea into the room. "The question is, what are *you* doing here?"

"Looking for Clara," I say as I lower the vase to my side.

"Well, *we* were looking for *you*," Amber says. "You totally freaked us out by taking off like that."

"Yeah," Drea says. "We were trying to keep up with you on the beach. We called out to you a couple times."

"You did?"

"Oh my god," Drea says, looking at the wall, at the words splotched across. "Is it blood?"

Amber shakes her head. "It's paint."

"How do you know?" I ask.

"The fumes. Definitely a water-based interior brand."

"I won't ask," Drea says.

"We need to call the police," I say. "Maybe they can get fingerprints or something."

"Yeah, but how are we supposed to explain why we're even in here?" Amber asks. "Hasn't anyone ever heard of *breaking and entering*? They'll think one of us did it."

"That's ridiculous," Drea says. "No one would *ever* think that one of us could possibly do something like that."

"Are you kidding?" Amber says. "It's so textbook. Girls cat-fighting over the same guy. One of them gets a little too possessive and starts with the death threats. She sneaks out of her room when everybody else is asleep to show just how peeved she is that Little Miss Hula Girl is trying to butter up on her bread."

"That's, like, *so* dumb." Drea huffs.

"It happens all the time," Amber says. "Don't you watch Lifetime?"

"You're obviously referring to yourself," Drea says, "what's the little jealousy thing you've got going with PJ and Clara?"

"I'm hardly jealous," Amber says. "And her name is Skank, not Clara."

"Hey, what's this?" I ask, picking a couple photos from the floor.

"What are they of?" Drea asks.

"Kind of hard to tell."

Amber takes and rotates them to get a better angle. "This one kind of looks like part of somebody's arm." She tilts her head for perspective. "And this one could be a forehead . . . but maybe it's a butt cheek."

"Photo duds." Drea sighs. "So what are we supposed to do now? Wait until Clara comes and finds this for herself?"

"I say we check the trash," Amber says, looking around the room for a wastebasket. "That's where all the dirt is."

"Literally," Drea says.

"No, seriously, that's where they find all the good clues on TV cop shows." Amber moves to the mirror to wipe away what's left of the aloe goo.

"I refuse to go trash-picking," Drea says, waving her thirty-dollar manicure at us.

"Fine," Amber says. "Let's just bug out of here then. We can wait for Clara to notice this on her own. No sense tying our asses to this mess."

"My ass already *is* tied to this mess," I say. "Have you forgotten about my nightmares . . . that something bad is going to happen to her? We need to find her. We need to stop thinking about ourselves for five minutes."

Drea nods. "Stacey's right . . . even if she is a cow."

"Fine," Amber says. "Let's go before I change my mind."

Amber returns the photo duds to the floor, beside the bed, while I set the vase back down on the night table and shut off the lights. It's better if the police see things exactly as they were left, which is why we also neglect to lock the door behind us.

We head back to our cottage, telling ourselves that Clara is going to be back there, that if she isn't we'll go straight to the police and tell them everything. We swing the door to the cottage open and, sitting on the couch, on top of the fitted sheet but under the knitted blanket that Drea lent her, is Clara, and she's got herself a little company.

She and Chad are facing one another, knee-to-knee, with actual kneecap touchage.

Chad looks at Drea and scoots back at least one full foot. "Hey, what are you guys doing? I thought you were in your room."

Clara giggles for no apparent reason and moves to cover her legs with the blanket. "Yeah," she says, "what are you guys doing up? Where did you go?"

"We should ask you the same thing," Drea says, folding her arms in front.

"Why?" Clara cocks her head, feigning confusion.

"I just came out to get some water," Chad says. He gestures to the coffee table, as though there's supposed to be a glass of water on it.

"Looks like you made a detour," Drea says.

"He saw I was a Bruins fan." Clara sticks her chest out, proudly displaying the team's white, black, and gold colors. "They're my lucky PJs."

"Where were you a little while ago?" I ask, interrupting her stupid giggle.

"What do you mean?" she asks.

"I came out here and you were gone."

More head-cocking. "Oh," she says, as though it just dawned on her. "I was in the bathroom for a while."

"Was it PJ's cooking?" Amber asks.

"No," she giggles. "I was washing my hair in the sink. I didn't want to take a full shower because I was afraid that would wake you guys up."

I nod, remembering how in my nightmare I went to the bathroom in search of Clara, how from just outside the door it sounded as though the sink faucet was running.

"That reminds me," Clara continues. "Drea, I brought you some Bumble & Bumble."

"Excuse me?"

"Bumble & Bumble . . . the hair conditioner . . . I thought it might be good for your split ends."

"I don't have split ends," Drea snaps. She grabs at a lock of hair, fanning out the individual strands for show.

"You don't?" Clara cocks her head for the umpteenth time. "Oops." She smiles. "Sorry, I guess it just kind of looks that way."

"Alrighty then," Amber interrupts. "Maybe we should all go back to bed before we wake up PJ and Jacob."

Chad stands up from the sofa and heads for the kitchen like nothing even happened.

"So that's it?" Drea asks him. "That's all you have to say for yourself?"

"What am I supposed to say?" He pulls a jug of water from the fridge. "The Bruins are my favorite team."

"It's my fault," Clara offers. She pulls her fingers through her dampened hair. "I just felt kind of chatty and wanted company. Chad was nice enough to chat with me. Hey, wait," she beams. "Get it? Chad . . . chat?"

"Are you drunk?" Amber asks her.

"Well, you can chat with Chad all night for all I care," Drea says.

"Don't do this," Chad says. "You're completely overreacting."

But despite Chad's pleas, Drea shoots him a dirty look, darts off into our room, and slams the door behind her.

"She isn't mad, is she?" Clara asks, her voice rising up for sincerity.

"No," Amber says. "She's pissed. Of course, I can't say I didn't tell her this would happen." Amber follows after Drea, leaving me to have to tell Clara about her room by myself. I look at Chad and he looks away, pretending to be thoroughly engrossed in guzzling water from the jug.

"Clara," I say, "we seriously need to have a talk."

"I'm sorry," she says, burying her face in her hands. "I didn't mean anything. I was only trying to be friendly."

Chad sticks his tail between his legs and, jug of water in hand, goes back to his room like he's not even hearing this.

I take a deep breath and glance at the clock. It's a little after three. Maybe a few more hours of sleep will make all the difference, will help us all be able to get our priorities straight and put things into perspective. "You're staying till morning, right?" I ask. "I mean, at least until nine or ten?"

"Of course," she says, wiping invisible tears. "Where would I go?"

"Good. I'll go and talk to them and then we'll discuss everything in the morning."

"Wait," she says. "Where did you guys go?"

"We'll talk about it later, okay?"

She nods, somewhat reluctantly, I think. I'm reluctant too. I almost can't believe I'm leaving things like this. But maybe, for now, it's for the best.

eighteen

I go back into our room and, just as expected, Amber and Drea are hardly in sleep mode. They're sitting on Amber's bed, amidst feather-fringed pillows and leopard-print linens, dishing about what a quote-unquote "skank" Clara is.

"They're my lucky PJs," Amber mocks. She giggles extra loud, cocks her head to the side, and pulls at the front of her T-shirt, making it look like she's got cones for boobs.

"Shhh," I say. "You're going to wake everybody up."

"I hate her," Drea says, lowering her voice. "I mean, *I hate her.*"

"Tell us how you really feel," I joke.

"I just can't believe her gall," Drea huffs. "After we allow her to sleep on *our* sofa."

"And eat *our* food," Amber hisses. "I spied her chowing a cannoli right before bed."

"May it go straight to her cow hips," Drea says.

"Why do you think she hides them under those stupid skirt-things she wears?"

"I hate her," Drea repeats. "And I hate Chad too." She plunges headfirst into one of Amber's pillows.

"I know," I whisper, sitting down opposite them on my bed. "The whole thing's heinous . . . but I still feel like we need to help her."

Drea recovers from her nosedive to look at me, her mouth hanging open in complete dismay. "Um, are you kidding? I'm not helping that house-wrecker."

"Don't you think you might be overreacting just a little?"

"Don't give me that Chad-speak," she says. "I saw what I saw. Plus, did you hear what she said about my hair?"

"I agree," Amber whispers. "We don't even know this girl."

"I know, but I really don't see where we have another choice. I mean, yeah, she's totally obnoxious and personally I think if I have to listen to her giggle one more time I just might snap, but we're talking about her life here. We *have* to help her."

"*We?*" Drea asks.

"Fine," I say, feeling my teeth clench.

"Don't be mad, Stacey," Amber says, "but you have to admit, it's not exactly easy to help someone who openly goes after your man."

"Wait," I say. "Are we talking about PJ right now or Chad?"

"What *is* it with you and PJ?" Drea asks her.

"It's quite simple," Amber whispers. "He sweats me; I reject him; everybody's happy."

"Except PJ," Drea says, checking her hair for split ends.

"I'm going to bed." I turn away to crawl beneath the covers.

"Jacob's next," Amber says to me. "Just you watch. First she ruined things between Casey and his girlfriend; then she starts flirting with PJ; then Chad . . . you gotta know he's next."

"I have a little bit more faith in Jacob than that," I snap. "And maybe I thought I could have a little faith in the two of you." I lie back against my pillow and turn away, thinking about the de-stressing spell we did yesterday, how they promised me I could rely on their friendship. I pull the covers up over my head. A couple seconds later, Drea comes and pulls them back down.

"You're not gonna just block us out," she says.

"Why not? That's what you're doing to me."

"I'm sorry, okay? But Amber's right; it's hard to feel sorry for someone who flirts with your boyfriend."

"And makes fun of your hair," Amber adds.

"So does that mean we're supposed to just let her die?" I sit back up.

Drea purses her lips and looks away. "No one said any-thing about dying."

"No," I say, "because I'm not going to let that happen—with or without your help."

"All right, already," Amber sighs. "We'll help the skank."

Drea nods in agreement, and I can't help but smile, even though a part of me still wants to be angry.

I spend the next several minutes telling them, in hushed tones, about the nightmare I had during the wee hours of this morning. We go over and over all the details, from Clara calling out to me to finding her body on the beach.

"That's so weird," Drea whispers. "Why would you dream about Clara having the bottle you threw out to sea?"

"Easy," Amber says. "It obviously means Clara's con-nected to the bottle, to the message inside."

"Yeah, but the message was different in my nightmare," I remind them.

"But the words weren't," Amber says. "I mean, you *did* say her voice said 'don't tell anyone' and 'if you tell I'll make you pay.'"

I nod. "But that's the part that bugs me. On the wall in her room, it just said 'I'll make you pay'. There was nothing about a secret." I grab the amulet from around my neck, not-ing how I should probably replenish the lavender oil inside.

"I wonder if it's somebody else's secret," Drea says. "I mean, maybe she knows something she shouldn't and somebody's threatening her about it."

"That's what I was thinking," I say. "But it doesn't make sense. If someone's threatening her over a secret, then why did he—"

"Or *she*—" Amber reminds us.

"Right," I say. "Why did *whoever* go through her underwear drawer?"

"Um, do I need to draw you a picture?" Amber asks.

"*You* went through Jacob's underwear drawer . . ." Drea offers.

"Yeah," I say, "but that was by accident. I never would have done that normally."

"Maybe I *should* draw you a picture," Amber says.

"Be serious," I say.

"Why do you think you're getting cold in your nightmares?" Drea asks.

"The loss of blood maybe."

"Yeah, but why is Clara bleeding? Is it a wound or something?"

I shake my head. "I don't know. I can't tell, but it seems like in each nightmare I have, the blood is more intense, like she's getting closer to death."

"Which means that your nosebleeds might get more intense, too," Drea points out.

I nod and glance down at my sheets. There's a tiny patch of dried blood from earlier this morning.

"You need iron," Amber pipes up. "And a multi-vitamin."

"A definite," I nod.

"Yeah," Drea says. "I mean, the last thing you'd want is to lose so much blood you start to get dizzy and stuff."

I nod in agreement, adding a trip to the drugstore for some vitamin supplements to my mental to-do list.

"What does Jacob say about all this?" Drea asks.

I shrug. "Just that he's here for me, that he wants to help me, that he knows I can do this."

"He's right," Drea says. "You *can* do this."

"I know. It's just . . . he's having nightmares, too."

"About what?" Amber asks.

I shake my head. "He won't tell me. At first I thought it was about Clara. You know—like that he could see something in her future that he didn't think I could handle. But now I don't know."

"Why won't he tell you?" Drea asks.

"I think it's because he thinks I have enough to worry about."

"I guess that makes sense," Drea says. "I mean, you have to admit, you have been on edge."

"An understatement," Amber coughs out.

"I know," I say, "but you also have to admit, it's not every day I have people's lives in my hands." Quite literally, I think, looking down at my fingers, picturing the splotches of blood across them from my nightmares.

"No," Amber says. "It's more like every year."

"Good point," I sigh. "But I also feel like there's more to my stress than Clara's life and Jacob's secrecy—something that I just can't—"

"You should trust him, Stacey," Drea continues. "Maybe he's just not ready to tell you every little thing. I mean, there are things in my past that I haven't told Chad."

"Do tell." Amber rubs her palms together for the dish.

"I don't know," Drea says. "Stupid stuff I tried; stuff I've thought about—embarrassing moments."

"Vague, vague, vague," Amber sings.

"The point is," Drea continues, "that even though I haven't told Chad these things, it doesn't mean I don't love him. Maybe I will tell him one day, or maybe I won't. But I think it would get pretty old if Chad kept hounding me about stuff I wasn't ready to share."

"Point taken," I say.

"Good, because I'll never admit to saying this, but don't think I haven't wished Chad felt for me a smidgen of what Jacob feels for you." Drea looks down at her hands, at her pink-and-white manicure and the bite marks she's made on one thumbnail.

I take her hand and squeeze it. "Chad loves you; I know he does."

"Yeah, he loves me, but it's different, you know? It's not the same as what you have with Jacob."

"At least you guys have boys to bitch about," Amber interrupts. "The last guy I dated was Superman over there." She gestures to her blow-up doll, suspiciously placed in the corner of the room beside her pleather belts and faux-fur boas. She gets up to fish inside the mini-fridge and pulls out not one but two containers of Ben & Jerry's. "To feed our funk," she says, handing us each a spoon.

We sit in a row on my bed, passing the containers of comfort back and forth, eating away at our gloom.

nineteen

After devouring all the ice cream left in our cottage, Amber, Drea, and I end up falling asleep for a couple more hours. When I get up, in lieu of taking a shower, I pull a halfway-clean T-shirt and a pair of shorts off the floor and head into the living room to talk to Clara. Once again, she isn't there.

Chad and Amber are sitting at the kitchen table eating breakfast and discussing the fraternity fundraiser cruise tomorrow night—basically, who should room with whom with respect to finances, significant others, and loud and obnoxious snoring.

"Are you going?" Chad asks me.

"Doubt it," I say, glancing toward the closed bathroom door and wondering if Clara's in there.

"Yeah, that's what Jacob said, too," Chad says.

"Really?"

He nods, licking what appears to be Danish goo from his fingers.

"Good," I say. "I'm glad we're on the same wavelength." Though a part of me wonders why Jacob didn't ask me himself. I chew the thought over with a bite of dry cereal straight out of the box, and then take another peek at the empty sofa. "Who's in the bathroom?"

"You need to ask?" Amber looks up at me, her face still red from the mud mask. "Who else takes over an hour to blow-dry her hair?"

"So where's Clara?"

"Who cares?" Amber moans. "I think my face is sizzling." She grabs a package of Popsicles and applies it to her cheek.

"The only thing that's going to make your face any less burnt is time, *real* aloe, and this." I grab a couple eggs from the fridge and crack them into a bowl, separating the yolks from the white parts.

"You've got to be kidding," she says.

"Hardly. Egg whites are famous in my family for treating burns and, since I didn't bring my aloe plant with me on vacation, it'll have to do." I direct Amber to tilt her head back.

Then I dip my fingers into the egg whites and smear the clear and pulpy mass down her face. The burn actually isn't that bad; it's more like a sunburn with a little bit of peeling on one cheek.

"Ahhh!" Amber moans in appreciation. "Who knew slimy rawness could feel this good? Wait," she pauses. "Let me rephrase."

"I think I just lost my appetite," Chad says.

"Then can I have what's left of your Danish?" Amber moves to nab it off his plate, but Chad is too quick. He takes a healthy bite and smiles at her as he chews. "Didn't your mother teach you to share?" she asks him.

"Didn't *your* mother teach you not to get egg on your face?"

"So hilarious," she says, rolling her eyes.

Chad takes another bite, getting a clump of the raspberry goo stuck in his facial scruff.

"What's that?" Amber asks. She leans forward and squints toward his face.

"What?" Chad rubs his chin.

"Is that a beard you're trying to grow?"

I pinch her in response, hoping she gets the message.

"I don't know," Amber continues. "It kind of looks like one. But maybe it's something else—dirt, *hair dye*, maybe."

Chad's mouth falls open, and I can't help but laugh out loud.

"What's that supposed to mean?" he asks.

"*Ooh la la*," PJ sings, emerging from his room, saving Amber from having to answer. "A little food fun for breakfast? Whatever it is, count me in."

"Is Clara with you?" I ask him.

He shakes his head.

"Well, then where is she?"

"Calm down," Amber says. "She probably just went out to stand on some street corner."

"This isn't funny." I move to the bathroom door and knock, just to be sure it isn't Clara in there.

"I'll be out in a minute," Drea snaps.

"She's been saying that for the past hour," Chad moans.

I peek back in our room, even though I know she's not there either. I go to the guys' room and knock lightly before peering in. Empty. "Where's Jacob?" I ask.

Amber shrugs and gets up, her face and hands glossy with egg whites. She looks out the front window and then goes outside, leaving the door wide open. Two minutes later she's back. "Found Clara!"

"Where?" I ask.

"Just like I said," Amber gloats. "Ho ho ho, merry Christmas."

"Is that supposed to make sense?" PJ asks.

"The skank's next door, flirting with Casey," Amber says. "How's that for clarity?"

"Seriously?" Chad asks.

"Boo hoo for you too," Amber gloats.

"She is not," PJ says. "You're just saying that because you're all dry and thorny."

"Horny, not thorny," Amber corrects. "But if you don't believe me, go have a look for yourself."

PJ does, and I follow right after him. We move out onto the front walkway and spot Clara right away. Only it looks as though she's doing a lot more floundering than flirting. She's standing on the frat guys' porch with Casey but she looks all distraught, waving her hands around, trying to explain something.

It doesn't appear as though Casey is buying the story. He ends up leaving her there, going back inside the cottage to get away.

Clara looks in our direction and spots us, which perks her right up. "Hey there!" she bubbles, trotting her way over. "Anyone up for breakfast?"

"What's going on?" PJ asks, completely straight-faced.

"What do you mean?" She cocks her head.

"What were you doing over there?"

"Oh," she giggles—the noise sending nails-on-a-chalkboard shivers down my spine. "I was just saying hi."

"It didn't look too friendly," I say. "I thought you two weren't speaking."

"Well, we aren't exactly. I just went to give my deposit money for the cruise. Are you guys going? I'm *so* excited."

"That's it?" PJ asks, ignoring the question.

"Well, I also went to smooth things over. I mean, I hate it when people are mad at me, especially when it isn't my fault."

"So did you?" I ask.

"Oh yeah," she says, adjusting the ties on her sarong—a candy-cane-striped one this time. "I mean, sort of."

"Well, *we* still need to talk," I say.

"Is something wrong?"

I nod.

"Well, it'll have to wait, my little Stacey Bee," PJ says, "because me and Miss Clara Bear have our own smoothing over and chit-chatting to do."

"Sorry," I say, linking arms with Clara, feeling a chill, even through her sweatshirt, radiate right down to the tips of my fingers. "My chit-chat takes priority." We leave PJ and walk down the beach strip toward her cottage.

"He's really cute." Clara giggles.

"He's really something, all right."

"So, I need to ask," she continues, "is Drea still mad?"

"She'll get over it."

"Me and Chad were just talking last night," she reminds me. "Nothing more."

I nod and bite at my bottom lip, fighting the urge to tell her that I wasn't born yesterday.

"So are they serious?" she asks.

"Excuse me?" I stop short and turn to look at her, wondering if I'm hearing things or if she's seriously asking me what I think she is.

"Chad and Drea," she clarifies. "At the Clam Stripper yesterday, she said they got in a fight. I was just wondering if they made up, if they're super serious or just kind of casual."

"Clara," I say, "I'm going to forget you asked that."

"Why?" Her eyebrows furrow up like she's thoroughly confused.

"Why?" I take a deep breath, swallowing down what I really feel like saying. "Because you have a lot more to worry about than boys."

Her mouth slides into a frown. "Does this have anything to do with where we're going?"

"We're going to your place," I say, guiding her in that direction again.

"Now?" Clara gasps. "What for?"

I nod, ignoring her other question. "Are your parents back yet?"

Clara shakes her head. "I doubt it. They said they were leaving around eightish, which means they probably won't get here until after noon."

"That's probably a good thing," I say. "At least for now."

"Why? What's going on? Is it something bad?"

I nod, knowing that I can't keep it from her, that in only a matter of minutes she'll see for herself.

"What is it?" She stops us again to study my face.

I keep my expression securely in check by looking away, focusing toward the shamrock-shaped clouds just ahead of us. I don't want to give too much away. I want her to see the words for herself. I need to see her reaction to them—if it might reveal that she knows who's after her. "You'll see," I say, moving forward again.

"I was actually planning on having you come over today," she says, trying to keep pace with me. "Just later. I mean, don't you think I should hang around your place for a little while . . . try and patch things up with Drea?"

"Well, I have a confession to make. I've already been to your place."

"*Huh?*" She stops. Her mouth drops open.

"When I couldn't find you early this morning, I thought that maybe you went back to your cottage."

"*And?*"

"And I went inside. *We* went inside—Drea, Amber, and me."

"*What?*" She gasps. "You guys went into my house? Without me? You just broke in?"

"The door wasn't locked, Clara. I was worried about you. We all were."

"So what happened? What did you see?"

"I'm sorry," I say, ignoring the questions. "I know—it was wrong. But if you knew me, you'd know; it's only because I thought you might be in danger. You *are* in danger," I remind her.

Clara studies me for several seconds. "What did you see?" she repeats.

Instead of answering, I look up at her cottage. It's just a house away now. "Let's go," I say, holding out my hand. Clara takes it and we climb the back steps, the bamboo wind chimes so loud and clamoring that I almost can't think straight. I wrap my hand around the doorknob, almost as though it's my house, and guide her inside.

We enter her room and Clara sees it right away. It looks even worse with the sunlight shining in through the windows. Clara starts trembling. Her stance begins to wobble a bit.

I help her to sit down on the bed and do my best to turn her away from it. But she can't stop looking. "Do you know who did this?" I whisper.

She swallows hard and shakes her head.

"Are you sure?"

She nods.

"Maybe someone who's angry at you, somebody who wants to try and scare you—"

"I told you, I don't know," she snaps. She flops back against her pillow, pulling the slack of covers up over her, revealing a large manila envelope, sitting beside her on the bed.

I pick up the envelope, trying to concentrate on the fibers, the way it feels in my hand.

Clara sits back up. "What is that?"

I shake my head, noticing the chill coming from the seal, the coolness of the edges.

"Oh my god," she says, her mouth trembling. "Where did you get that?"

"It was on your bed, under the covers."

I bring the envelope up to my nose. It smells like butterscotch. Like her.

"What is it?" Clara asks. "What's wrong?"

"It smells like you," I say.

"What does that mean? It was in my bed."

"I know. It's just, whatever's in here . . . I feel like it captures you in some way."

Clara covers her eyes and rubs her forehead. "I don't want to know, okay? I don't want to see what's inside. You look and then just tell me if it's bad."

"Okay," I say, knowing already that it is bad. I turn away and tear at the flap, the envelope getting colder in my hands by the moment, like my skin is icing over just holding it. I peek inside and see a stack of Polaroids, reminding me of the ones that Amber found earlier. I look down at the floor by the bed. They're still there—a picture of an almost-arm and a possible butt-cheek.

"What is it?" Clara asks. She's looking at me now.

I reach inside the envelope and pull out the photos. They're pictures of Clara, at least thirty of them. They're all taken, it seems, from outside various windows of her cottage—Clara pulling off her sweatshirt, changing into her shorts, getting ready to take a shower, wearing only a towel . . .

"Tell me!" she demands.

I look at her and bite my bottom lip. "We should call the police."

"Show me!" Clara holds her hands out for the pictures. "I have to see."

"Are you sure?"

She pauses a moment before nodding.

I hand them to her and watch as she flips through each one—as her mouth trembles and her chin shakes. After seeing about ten, she throws them down on the bed and clenches fistfuls of pillow fabric.

"It'll be okay," I say, sitting down beside her. I pick up the other photos, the ones from the floor. "It looks like whoever left these dropped a couple."

"*What?*" Clara grabs them from me.

I peek over her shoulder at the pictures, trying to make out blurs of peach mixed with globs of red and brown.

"It's like they're playing games with me," Clara snivels. "Nobody makes mistakes like this. Nobody puts photos in an envelope, puts it in your bed, and then happens to drop some on the floor." She clenches the pillows harder, her knuckles turning to bone.

"It'll be okay," I say. "Just breathe. We'll get through this." I pluck a tissue from the box beside her bed and blot the tears that stream down her cheeks.

Clara takes a giant breath, blowing out her mouth, trying to calm herself down. After several moments and even more tissues, she seems just a little bit stronger, more stable. She looks at me and tries to smile, her hands letting up a bit from the clench-hold on her pillow. "I'm sorry," she says.

"For what?"

"It's just that I hardly know you. I'm not usually like this."

"Of course not," I say, patting her forearm. "I mean, this isn't exactly the most usual of circumstances. It's not every day you come home to—"

"That," she finishes, looking up at the words again.

"Hey," I say, turning her face away from it. "You need to be strong. You need to call the police. Get them over here. Have them see everything."

Clara nods and grabs the phone.

"Wait," I say, pausing her from dialing. "Do you think it might have been that photographer guy next door?"

"I don't know," she says. "I hadn't really thought about it . . . maybe."

The idea of it seems to upset her even more. She nearly bites through her cheek and resumes dialing. It takes her a couple times to actually get her jittery fingers to work right. "Hello," she stammers into the receiver. "My name is Clara Baker. I'm vacationing at 24 Sandy Beach Lane. I need you to come right away." She pauses a moment to stare into my eyes. "Because someone wants to kill me."

twenty

In practically less time than it takes me to stuff the photos back inside the envelope, to try once more to sense something from them through touch, the police arrive. Clara does all the talking, which both surprises and impresses me. I think it's healthy that she's talking about everything, taking things seriously, and being proactive.

She leads them through the living room and into her room, telling them how we came in here this morning and saw the graffiti on the wall, and then how we found the envelope of photos stuffed beneath her bed covers. But what's weird is that she fails to tell them how Amber, Drea, and I were actually here earlier this morning—how that's when *we* saw the message on the wall.

I look at it, at the blood-red words sprawled across the wall, wondering if Clara's intentionally leaving that detail out, if maybe she's trying to protect us. I guess, as Amber pointed out last night, it *would* look kind of suspicious for us. I cringe just thinking how openly Drea and Amber have expressed sheer loathing for Clara. If the police started asking questions about that, about whether all of us got along as friends, after hearing that the three of us broke in here, it might not look too good for us.

So, while I can understand why Clara might be protecting me, I'm wondering why she'd bother protecting them. Unless, of course, the detail just slipped her mind. I ponder that possibility a moment, but then Clara looks directly at me. "Stacey," she says, her face all flushed, "I'd really like to speak to the police alone now." She grabs a tissue from the box and dabs her eyes. The two police officers stare at me— one woman with dark, slicked-back hair that curls around her ears, and an older skinny guy with tiny round glasses.

"Oh," I say, taken aback completely.

"But I'll come over after," Clara says. "We can talk more then."

I nod and look at the police, wondering what she's going to tell them. The female officer takes my name, address, and telephone number, and tells me she might need to talk to me some more later—even though I didn't get to say much at all.

So now what?

I head back to the cottage, eager to hear back from Clara—to see what else she said to the police, to see if they might have said something insightful to her. Though now, after being asked to leave just as the questioning was starting to heat up, I know I can't rely solely on her for information. There's obviously stuff she doesn't want to tell me.

I enter the cottage, and Jacob is sitting at the kitchen table eating a bagel. "Where have you been?" he asks.

"I could ask you the same."

"What do you mean?"

"When I got up this morning, you'd already left."

"I went for an early swim."

I look toward his swim trunks. "Then how come your bathing suit is dry? How come your hair isn't wet?"

"It's practically ninety degrees out, Stacey. It doesn't take much for something to dry."

I nod, trying to decide whether or not to believe him.

"So?" he asks again. "Where were you?"

"With Clara," I say. "Talking to the police."

"What happened?"

"Total bust." I sigh, leaning back against the door.

"Are you okay?"

"Fine. Tired. Hungry."

"Will a bagel make it better?"

"Only if it has extra strawberry jam."

Jacob gets up and pops a frozen one into the toaster oven for me. He pours me a glass of iced coffee, adds in a little cream—just the way I like it—and sets it on the kitchen table beside the jar of strawberry preserves.

"Perfect," I say, already feeling a smidge better. "Thank you."

"Sure," he says, sitting back down at the table. "So?"

"What?"

"What happened? I heard about the graffiti on Clara's wall and how you went over there to show her."

Plate in hand, I position myself beside the toaster oven, waiting for the ping. "There were pictures, too," I say. "Polaroids of Clara—a whole envelope of them."

"Were you able to sense anything from them?"

I shrug. "Just more of the same—coldness, chills. But I was also able to sense *her;* it was like I could smell her, her butterscotch scent."

"Well, they *were* photos of her."

"I know. It probably doesn't mean anything. The whole thing's a puzzle." I take the bagel out and join him at the table for some much-needed fueling.

"Maybe some ex of hers did this," Jacob says. "Maybe someone she might have upset . . . someone who may have thought she was cheating? I mean, she does seem kind of—"

"Flirty?"

"Well, now that you mention it."

"You've obviously been talking to Drea and Amber," I say, spreading on a thick layer of jam.

"Actually, I was talking to Chad. He said she really came on to him last night."

"And he was a helpless victim?" I take a bite of my bagel, noticing right away that the center is still cold from the freezer. But my stomach has been growling for at least the past hour, so with the sweetness of the jam, I don't even care.

"I'm not saying he was a victim," Jacob continues. "It's just that we *know* Chad. We don't exactly know Clara."

"And what does that mean? Just because I don't know Clara that well, I'm not going to help her?" I get up and grab a stream of paper towels from the roll and a red dry-erase marker from the board on the fridge. At the top of the paper towels, I write Clara's name. Then, below it, I write the words I'LL MAKE YOU PAY, trying to make it look like it did on her wall—the pointed capital letters, the *K* and the two *Ys* the most pronounced. I concentrate a moment on the color, wondering why someone chose to use red paint, if it has any significance.

But I just don't know. I can't seem to think straight. I push the towels to the side and resume eating breakfast, hoping a little food energy will help do the trick.

"That's not what I'm saying at all," Jacob continues. He eyes the paper towels, my attempt to make sense of the message. "I think you *should* help Clara."

"Then what?"

"It's all about trust."

"Well, obviously Clara doesn't trust me enough to tell me everything. And why should she? It's not like I haven't broken into her house behind her back." I take a sip of iced coffee, hoping to cool the agitation I feel boiling up inside me. I mean, why am I feeling all defensive? It's obvious that Clara *does* have a flirting fetish. I mean, between Casey, PJ, and Chad . . . and those are just the guys we know about. "I'm sorry," I say, finally. "I'm just frazzled."

"It's okay." Jacob reaches across the table to take my hand, not even minding that my fingers are sticky from jam. "You're not alone on this, Stacey. I'm willing to help you. I *want* to help you."

"I know."

"Then why don't we do a spell together? Something to help us focus on Clara, on the graffiti message, the photos, or the cold vibrations you've been getting." He squeezes my hand and concentrates on me hard, making my heart do that ratta-tap-tapping thing; I picture it like a cartoon, when the giant red animated heart starts pumping out of the character's chest.

"Maybe I just need a little break."

"Anything particular in mind?"

"How does an overnight frat cruise sound?"

"Are you serious?" he asks, his eyebrows arched high for surprise.

"Chad told me you didn't want to go."

"And you *do?*"

"I just thought you might have asked me."

"Sorry," he says. "It just didn't sound like your type of thing."

"It isn't, but I might have to go anyway."

"Why?"

"Clara. I think she might be going and, if she is, I should probably plan on going as well."

Jacob looks away, completely avoiding the unspoken question.

"Well?" I ask.

"What?"

"Tell me you'll go, too."

"I don't know," he sighs. "It sounds kind of lame."

"Yeah, but if I have to be there—"

"I don't know," he repeats.

"Are you serious? We can get our own room. We can think of it as some time away to ourselves."

"How?" he asks. "You're going to be too busy with Clara."

"Not the whole night. Plus, I can make sure she gets a room right next to ours."

"Maybe," he says, finally.

"Don't sound *so* enthusiastic."

"It's just—"

"Just think about it, okay?" I reach across the table to clasp his fingers again.

He nods and smiles at me, and I feel my cheeks warm over. I'm just about to get up and plant the most delicious kiss across his lips when I hear a knock at the door. I get up to answer it.

It's the police.

The same two officers from Clara's cottage stand in front of me, flashing their badges in plain view. "Stacey Brown?" the female cop says. "We need to talk to you about your visit to Clara's cottage earlier this morning. Are your friends," she checks her notepad again, "Amber and Drea available for some questions?"

I look back at Jacob, and he stands from the table. "They went out," he says.

"Do you know where they went?" the other cop asks.

Jacob shakes his head, still focusing on me.

"We're not in any kind of trouble," I ask, "are we?"

"We need to talk to all three of you," the female cop says, failing to answer my question.

"Well, it's just me right now," I say. "Will that do?"

"For now."

"Fine," I say, looking back at Jacob. "Let's get started."

twenty-one

Since I haven't exactly been charged with anything yet—including breaking and entering, of which I am totally-and-without-a-doubt guilty—the police try and keep things as casual as possible; at least it seems like they're keeping things casual. They don't insist that we head down to the station to discuss the details, but rather they suggest that we go over things in the quiet of our living room.

I'm just hoping Amber and Drea stay away until after I'm done.

I introduce Jacob, and he takes a seat beside me on the sofa, on the bed linens and blanket still set up from Clara's stay. He reaches over to hold my hand, pumping it a couple times to remind me that he's here, that I'm not alone.

"So," the female officer says, eyeing around the room. Her gaze pauses on the paper towels lined up at the edge of the kitchen table, where I wrote Clara's name as well as the message from her bedroom wall in the bright-red marker. She looks at them and then at me, the words clearly legible.

I cough as though that might distract her a moment, make the words go away. But it doesn't. And they don't. So she just stares at me, waiting for me to break—for the walls all around us to come crashing down. When none of that happens, she resumes her questioning. "Clara mentioned that you went into her cottage early this morning when she wasn't at home. Is that correct?"

I nod. "But it was only because I was looking for her. She was staying with us last night, and when I woke up and saw that she wasn't here, I got worried and went to look for her. I thought that maybe she went back to her cottage for something. The door wasn't locked."

The other cop stares at me from behind those microscopic glasses. I make an effort to smile at him, to break the tension, but his face remains expressionless.

"And what time was that?" the cop-lady continues.

"I don't know," I say. "Around 2:30 maybe."

She jots the detail down in her notepad. "Did you see anyone coming in or going out of Clara's cottage at that time?"

I shake my head and proceed to answer the rest of her questions—questions that detail how Amber and Drea came in afterwards; how they had been looking for me since I ran out of our cottage all a-tizzy; how no, we didn't see the envelope of photos at the time, but yes, we did notice the graffiti; and no, we have absolutely no idea who could have done this.

She pauses a few moments to jot down some notes, the end of her ballpoint pen bobbing back and forth with vigor. "I don't suppose," she flips a page back in her notebook, "that Chad is around for some questions?"

I shake my head, wondering how she even knows about Chad. I mean, what did Clara say to her about him? "Why would you want to talk to him? I mean, he was sleeping when we went to Clara's this morning."

"I can attest to that," Jacob says. "He, PJ, and I share the same room."

"And at no time during the night did you hear one of your roommates get up?"

"Well, just once," Jacob says.

Here we go. *What* is Jacob thinking? I squeeze his hand extra hard, trying to wrangle him to his senses.

"Who?" she asks.

"I think Chad might have gotten up once for some water, but that's normal for him. He gets up frequently during the night."

"Because of the water," I add, as though she needs the explanation.

"Do you know what time he might have gotten up?" she asks.

Jacob shakes his head and squeezes my hand, perhaps letting me know that he's sorry for saying something in the first place. The other cop notices. He looks up at me—deep into my eyes as though he's not buying any of this.

"Well, that will be all for now," she says. She takes one last look at the paper towels, one penciled-in eyebrow raised high for effect. "But we'll probably be in touch." She hands me her card and tells me to have Drea and Amber give her a call when they get back.

The two officers leave, and Jacob and I just look at each other. "What just happened?" I ask him.

Jacob shakes his head, completely baffled as well.

twenty-two

As soon as the police leave, Jacob and I head over to the Clam Stripper to look for everybody. Part of me wants to wait around for Clara, to find out what she said to the police, though I'm not so sure she'd tell me. It's obvious that if she wanted me to know, she wouldn't have made me leave in the first place.

I press the sea-glass amulet between my fingers and breathe the salt air in, concentrating on the sound of the waves as they rush against the sand, trying to remind myself that clarity comes with mindfulness. I need to keep a level head.

Jacob reaches for my hand, as though sensing my mounting anxiety. "We'll figure this out," he says. "The police are just doing their job."

I nod, telling myself that that's true—that obviously they had to come and talk to us. I mean, we *did* break into Clara's house. We *were* the first ones to see the graffiti on her wall. For all she could know, we're the ones who did it.

I take a deep breath and lead us onto the Clam Stripper deck. Amber is the first to spot us since it seems Chad and Drea are too busy making up. They're sitting at the picnic table, so close to one another that you couldn't even squeeze a measly French fry between them. There's a small box of Godiva chocolates—Drea's favorites—with a pink ribbon sitting on the table in front of her. It's the telltale sign that the happy couple was in a fight, and that Chad is trying to patch things up.

"Hey guys," she says, resting her head against Chad's shoulder. She looks up at us for about half a second before focusing back on Chad—kissing his cheek and nuzzling her forehead against his chest.

"Someone get these two a room." Amber sighs.

"How about we get ourselves a room instead?" PJ goes to drape his arm around Amber, but she pushes him away.

"I'm nobody's sloppy seconds," she says.

"You guys," I say, cutting through their banter. "We need to talk."

"What's up?" Chad asks, pausing from a smooch.

"The police were just at our place. They questioned me about going to Clara's, about seeing the graffiti. They also want to talk to you guys."

"All of us?" Drea asks.

"Well, everyone except PJ and Jacob." I continue to tell them the details about the questioning and how Clara didn't want me to hear what she said to the police. I also tell them about the envelope full of Clara photos I found underneath her bed covers.

"Why would they want to talk to Chad?" Drea asks. "He wasn't even with us this morning when we went to her place."

"I know," I say, "but they didn't give me any details."

Drea looks thoroughly concerned for him. She kisses his cheek yet again, as though the fact that the three of us are being questioned is completely irrelevant.

"It's probably just routine," I say, finally taking a seat. "We shouldn't jump to conclusions."

"Stacey's right," Jacob says. "We need to talk to Clara."

"I knew that skank was trouble." Amber tosses a fry down on the table.

I look at PJ, wondering if he's going to try and defend Clara, but he doesn't. We continue to discuss the whole predicament for several more minutes, until the conversation at our table comes to an unexpected halt.

"Hey guys!" Clara giggles.

I turn around and there she is, practically out of nowhere, standing behind our table.

"Where did *you* come from?" Chad asks.

Drea shoots him a dirty look, as though he's not even supposed to talk to her.

"I went by your place, but nobody was home. Are you here for brunch or lunch?" She nervous-giggles and looks at her watch.

"How did it go with the police?" I ask, cutting through her question.

"And how come you kicked Stacey out while you talked to them?" Amber plucks a fry from the box and evil-eyes Clara.

Clara's smile wilts in response. She looks at me. "Sorry about that. It's just . . . I wanted to talk to them alone."

"Why?" Drea asks.

Clara shrugs. "I wanted to tell them about my ex-boyfriends and stuff. I don't know, I guess I didn't want anyone to hear all that bad stuff."

"Is that who you think is doing all this?" I ask her.

Clara looks away, her cheeks all flushed. "I don't know. It's kind of hard to imagine anyone I know doing stuff like this, especially someone I might have been seeing." She makes an effort to smile, but I think she can sense everyone's reluctance toward her. While Amber sizes her up, Drea cuddles in closer toward Chad, marking her personal territory.

"Are your parents back yet?" I ask her.

"Finally. My mom is totally flipping over this. They came home while I was talking to the police—right at the end."

"So you've told them everything."

She gives a slight nod and looks away again, like maybe she isn't telling the truth—at least not the *complete* truth.

"Well, at least you won't be staying alone now."

"So maybe we can get together later," she says, changing the topic. She looks toward PJ, but he hasn't so much as peeped in her direction once. She turns to Chad. "What do you say? Sound good? We could go hang out downtown. There's this cool surf shop with tons of boards, if you're into that."

"Why do the copsters want to talk to me and Drea?" Amber asks, ignoring her suggestions.

"They *do?*" Clara cocks her head in confusion.

"The police came by our place a little while ago," I explain.

Her eyebrows furrow as though she's thoroughly perplexed. "I might have mentioned that you guys saw the graffiti before I did, but I didn't make it sound weird or anything. I said you guys were looking for me and thought I went home. I told them the door wasn't locked."

"And now they think we did it," Amber says, batting her eyelashes at Clara.

"I'm sorry," Clara says. "I don't know—"

"Why do they want to talk to Chad?" Drea asks, interrupting her.

Clara shakes her head and bites her lip, her eyes extra wide.

"I have to go," Jacob says, amidst all this—like it couldn't get any worse.

"Where?" I ask.

"There's something I have to do." He smiles slightly, as though that's supposed to assure me, make it all okay.

"Like what? We're on vacation; what could you possibly have to do?"

He gets up. "We'll talk about it later, okay?"

"I thought we might go swimming . . ."

"Later," he says, kissing my cheek. I watch him walk away, just like that, and feel my heart start to crumble up.

"Maybe he's got cramps," Amber says, replacing the sweat-drenched tissues in her cleavage with a couple fresh napkins.

Drea reaches across the table to squeeze my forearm, obviously sensing my disappointment. She pries open the box of chocolates. "Dig in," she says. "They're best when they're melty like this."

"No, thanks."

"Maybe I should go, too," Chad says. He gets up and taps PJ on the shoulder, gesturing for him to give us a little girl time as well.

"Should I leave, too?" Clara asks when it's just the four of us. Her face is all red, like maybe she's sensing her own awkwardness.

I shake my head and glance down at my amethyst ring, knowing that I need to keep my priorities straight, that Clara's life depends on it. "No," I say. "If misery loves company, I think you've definitely come to the right place. Speaking for myself, of course."

"Guys can be such jerks," Amber says, turning to me.

"Is that why all your dates are inflatable?" Drea asks her.

"For real?" Clara giggles.

"At least they're not *taken*," Amber snaps.

Clara ignores the comment. She takes a seat beside Drea on the bench, causing Drea to stiffen up a bit.

"Is Jacob still being all negative about the cruise?" Amber asks.

I nod. "He definitely doesn't want to go . . . not that I do."

"So you two are having problems?" Clara's eyes suddenly widen.

I shake my head since I really don't feel like getting into the complexities of my love life with her, of all people.

"He's so mysterious," Clara beams. "I mean, if you don't mind my saying so. I think that's a good thing, you know? Kind of sexy."

I shrug.

"He was telling me last night how when you guys first started dating, you were much more relaxed."

"Excuse me?"

"He just thinks you've been kind of uptight lately. Have you been? I mean, I guess you have reason to be—considering the nightmares and all."

I feel my mouth drop open. "When were you talking to him?"

"Last night. Well, actually, this morning. After you guys came back from my cottage, you went back to bed, but I stayed up for a little while. So when Jacob got up to go out, he saw that I was awake, and we just started chatting. I hope I haven't said something wrong. I mean, we only talked for a couple of minutes. He's really into you. Trust me; you have nothing to be worried about."

I'm looking at her, watching as she nods emphatically, wondering how she can sit here and pretend to be an expert on my relationship.

"He has a dark side, though, doesn't he?" she continues. "I mean, he always seems like he's hiding something. So mysterious." There's a huge glowing smile across her face, like all of this is a compliment.

I feel my jaw quiver just imagining Jacob talking to her, just imagining him opening up to her this way, when he's been anything but open with me. "I don't feel so good."

"What's wrong?" Clara asks.

"Are you serious?" Amber narrows her eyes at Clara. "I mean, are you seriously that—"

Drea pokes a chocolate into Amber's mouth. "We should probably get going." She stands up from the table, gesturing for me to join her.

"We'll talk later," I tell Clara. "Right now I'm just not feeling too well."

Clara nods like she understands, like she knows better than to believe that my feeling ill is the result of a headache, the heat, or something I ate, but right now I just don't care. I need to get away.

twenty-three

After Amber and Drea reiterate their utter loathing for Clara, reminding me that Jacob may be next in her long line of summer diversions, the two head off to talk to the police, to get it over with once and for all. Meanwhile, I go back to the cottage to see if I can find Jacob, to see what was up with his needing to get away. But, as I might have guessed, he isn't around.

But Chad is.

"Hey," he says, lifting his sunglasses to the top of his head. He's wearing a pair of swim trunks, bright pumpkin-colored ones, with neon-yellow stripes that run down the sides. "What's up?"

I shake my head and look away.

"You can't lie to me, Stacey," he says. "I know you, re-member?"

"I'm just not feeling well."

"With good reason," he says. "What's up with Jacob lately?" He takes a seat on the couch and looks up at me for some response.

"What do you mean?"

"I don't know. He's been acting kind of weird, don't you think . . . sort of distant?"

I plunk down on the sofa next to him. "I'm glad you noticed it, too."

"Yeah," Chad says. "What's going on with him? Are you guys fighting?"

"No. At least I don't think we are."

"O-kay," he says with a quizzical look.

"It's just confusing, I mean . . . all this relationship stuff. Just when you think everything's perfect—it isn't." I look away, feeling my eyes fill up. I hate myself for crumbling this way in front of Chad—my ex-boyfriend, of all people.

"I wouldn't worry about it too much," he says, reaching out to touch my shoulder. "It's probably just something he's going through right now."

"So why won't he go through it with me?"

"Who knows? Guys can be pretty cryptic sometimes, es-pecially when it comes to relationship stuff. Just ask Drea.

Sometimes I don't know why she keeps coming back to me."

"You're not so bad."

"And neither are you." He smiles at me, and I bite my lip, my cheeks feeling suddenly flushed.

"Thanks," I say.

"Sure." He leans in to hug me, and I hug him back, closing my eyes in the embrace. It feels so good to hold him like this—as friends. So long overdue. When we broke up last year—when he started dating Drea and I started seeing Jacob—I think we all tried to pretend that it wasn't completely awkward to stay friends. Even though sometimes—a lot of the time—it really was.

"Hey," Jacob says, startling us. He moves into the living room from the hallway.

"Where did *you* come from?" I ask, looking down the hallway toward his bedroom. I scoot up on the sofa, breaking my embrace with Chad.

"Out."

"Out *where?*" I ask.

"I should let you two talk." Chad gets up from the sofa. He flips his sunglasses down over his eyes, grabs his beach towel off the back of the kitchen chair, and heads outside.

"So?" I ask, looking back at Jacob.

"I had to take care of something."

"What?"

He takes a seat beside me on the sofa. "Why are you getting all upset?"

"I just thought we were going to spend some time together. I wanted to go swimming."

Jacob takes my hands, sandwiching them between his own. "I'm sorry. Let me make it up to you."

I feel myself getting tenser by the moment, the pit in my chest getting bigger, harder to breathe away. I bite my lip to keep from losing it, fully aware that he's avoiding the question. "How come you didn't tell me you talked to Clara last night?"

"Clara?"

I nod and suck in my lips.

"We all talked to her."

"No," I say. "She told me you talked to her after we all went to bed."

Jacob's eyebrows rise up like he's genuinely surprised.

"She said you went out early this morning after we got back from her place," I continue. "She said you guys talked about how uptight I am, how when we first started dating I was much more relaxed."

"Stacey—"

"Did you?"

"I went for a walk on the beach—"

"At 3 AM?"

"I don't know, I didn't check the clock . . . maybe. But I didn't stop and talk with Clara."

"Not at all?"

"I might have said hi. I might have asked if she was comfortable, if she needed anything."

"Then how did she know those things? She knew how long we'd been dating."

"She could have found that out from anyone." He squeezes my hands tighter. "You need to trust me. I trust *you.*"

"I don't give you a reason not to."

"And I do?"

I shrug, hating myself for being this way, for feeling so insecure. "What am I supposed to think? You say you went out for a 3 AM walk, but then you weren't even around first thing this morning when we all got up."

"It's not what you're thinking."

"And what *am* I thinking?"

"I don't know—that I never came back after my walk; that I'm seeing someone else, maybe. How can you even think those things? You know how I feel about you."

I take a deep breath, not wanting to repeat myself, not wanting to sound like an insecure nag.

"I could have gotten jealous about you and your ex-boyfriend," he continues, "cuddling up on the sofa a few minutes ago."

My first response is to lash out at him, especially since Chad was so understanding with me, since he also noticed that Jacob's been acting weird. But I swallow my anger and, instead, ask the question that seems most obvious to me. "And did you?"

"Did I what?"

I concentrate on his eyes, knowing that I'll be able to tell if he isn't honest. "Did you get jealous of Chad and I just now?"

Jacob gives me yet another surprised look, his eyes widening. "No."

I feel my lower lip tremble at the ease of his response. "Maybe that's the problem," I say, breaking his grip on my hands. I get up from the couch, my fingers clamped around my amulet necklace.

"Where are you going?" he asks.

"I have some stuff to do," I say, hoping that I sound as secretive as he does. I retreat to my room, closing the door behind me.

twenty-four

I try calling my mother for a much-needed dose of maternal comfort, but I just get the machine. Fabulous. But even more fabulous is that I'm too depressed to bother leaving a message, and so I just hang up. Honestly, I don't think I could feel any worse. I hate being the bad guy in the relationship, and yet I don't know what else to be. I mean, I *do* trust Jacob—more than anything. But I can't help feeling this way. I can't help feeling somewhat jilted that he's keeping things from me, that he won't let me into his world completely. That he's possibly talking about the problems in our relationship with people he doesn't even know.

I mean, when I really stop and think about it, I don't think I have one solitary secret that Jacob doesn't know about. So maybe that's my problem. Or maybe it's the moon, the pull it has on me this week, making me feel all off-balance. I don't know; I'm just feeling so completely unhinged. I almost feel like the stress I have about helping Clara is one of the easier things I have to deal with—which, despite the boost of confidence I've had as far as that matter is concerned, isn't saying much.

I open the door of my room and look around the cottage for Jacob, but it seems he's already gone out. Great. What I should really be doing is hitting the sheets, trying to score myself a little shuteye so I can dream. But since I can't even think about falling asleep right now, I move into the bathroom for a shower, hoping the warm water coupled with steam and bath oil will help relax me a bit.

Standing in the mirror, my hair looks about as frazzled as I feel, if not worse—like the what-not-to-do picture in a magazine. The ends are all dry and frayed from the sun, from not taking the time to pamper myself properly.

I grab my bowl of flower petals from the window. It's full of roses, lilac buds, and hydrangea bits. Using a funnel, I drain the cup of water I added to the bowl last night into my half-empty bottle of shampoo. I shake the bottle to mix it all up. It's a recipe my grandmother swore by to give hair life and luster—and to help enliven one's spirit, since I'm feeling so completely depleted. The sweet rosy scent mixed with the lilacs and my dandelion shampoo does help to perk me up a bit.

I turn on the shower faucet and step inside the tub, thinking how my grandmother used to stress the importance of cleansing as a way to prepare the body for a spell. I spend a good twenty minutes doing just that, imagining myself washing away the negative energy and restoring my inner peace.

Feeling much more balanced, I slip into a robe and go back to my room. I wonder if all of what Clara said about her talk with the police is true—if she really did tell them about her ex-boyfriends, if she thinks one of them is responsible. But then why did they want to talk to Chad? What does he have to do with anything? I rack my brain for an answer, wondering what Clara might have said. I wouldn't be so suspicious if the police wanted to talk to Jacob and PJ as well, but singling Chad out like this—it just doesn't make sense.

I pull a pad of notebook paper and a yellow crayon from my night table, wondering if Casey is indeed Clara's ex-boyfriend. According to him, it's like they barely even know each other, but she makes it sound as though they had some secret relationship going. I write the word "TRUTH" across the paper, hoping the yellow color of the crayon will help promote clarity, hoping my dreams will slice through all these contradicting stories of he-said versus she-said.

I fold the paper up, whispering the word "truth" with every crease, until it's a tiny paper ball that I slip underneath my pillow. I pull my spell-supply suitcase from under my bed and take out my hourglass. Tall and slender, made out of real cut glass with full-blown bulbs at each end, I position it on my night table and watch as the sparkly white sand inside filters down into the bottom bulb. I grab my dream box and position it open over my heart center. Then I lie back against my pillow, concentrating on the idea of time. I need to know how much time I have before Clara is going to die.

I close my eyes, still picturing the sands as they fill up the bottom of the hourglass, feeling more relaxed by the moment. The sultry ocean breeze filters in through the window screen, filling the room with the scent of coconut mixed with seashells, easing me to sleep.

twenty-five

After my nap, I decide to take that swim I've been thirsting for. I change into my bathing suit, grab a towel, and head out. What's weird is that despite the prime swimming hour, there isn't anybody on the beach. I walk a bit farther down the strip, seeing if I can spot Jacob somewhere, wondering if he might be over at the Clam Stripper. But that's empty, too. The order and pick-up windows are boarded up, and the picnic tables are missing, as well. It's almost like I've been fast-forwarded to winter mode, which actually might explain why I'm feeling so cold, why goosebumps have sprouted up all over my skin.

I decide to head into the bathroom to warm up. The public bathroom is in the center of the parking lot. It's basically this houselike brick structure with showers attached to the outside of the building. I go around to the ladies' room entrance and try the door, thinking how normally it's left wide open, wondering why everything is closed up today. The door budges a little, but it seems like it's caught on something.

I pull a little harder on the handle, using both hands this time. Finally it tugs open, causing me to stumble back. I take a step inside, noticing how spacious it is without people standing in line for a stall. It's dark, the only light coming in through a tiny window above the sink area. I look around for a light but can't seem to find one. Instead, I spot one of those wooden doorstoppers. I wedge it into the crack at the bottom of the door, allowing the light from outside to paint a streak across the floor.

I take a few steps farther inside, moving around to the left where all the stalls are, noticing how the green concrete flooring is all muddy from beach sand mixed with water. The sinks are dripping; there's a puddle on the floor underneath them from leaking pipes. I move to the sink in the corner, the only one that doesn't seem to have a drippy faucet. I turn the valve on so that the warm water washes down over my fingers, and then I splash a couple times on my face. That's when I hear the outer door slide closed, despite the door wedge—leaving me in the dark.

"Hello?" I look over my shoulder toward the doorway. "Can you open the door back up?"

But no one answers, and the door remains closed.

I peer up toward the window above me, but it's really too small to allow much more than a strip of light across the mirror and sinks. Someone's foot scratches against the sandy concrete floor; I can hear the shifting. I stand frozen in place and look up into the mirror, waiting to see whoever it is.

"Hello?" I call again.

But instead I just hear giggling, like someone's playing a joke on me. Slowly, I move around the corner toward the door, noticing that the farther I get from the window, the darker it becomes.

"Are you looking for me?" a voice whispers.

I stop, a shiver running down the back of my neck. "Clara?" I ask, recognizing the voice.

"Clara's dead," she says, giggling. "You let her die."

"No." I shake my head, reminding myself to breathe, to be strong. I take a couple more steps, but it's completely dark in front of the door. I hold my arms out in front of me, my fingers trembling from how cold I feel, and search for the door handle. But I can't find it. Instead I find something else. It hangs midair in front of the door. I wrap my hands around it and feel my thumb get pricked, like a needle. I gasp, rubbing my fingers together, feeling a bit of moisture. I must be bleeding. I poke my thumb into my mouth and then reach for the object again. There are pins that stick through the center of something soft and rubbery. Carefully, I move my hands up and feel cloth. I move them up a little more and feel hair of some sort. Like a doll.

"For you, Stacey," whispers the voice. It's coming from where the door is, but I can't see anything.

My heart is thrashing inside my chest. I go to take the doll-like figure, noticing how it's hanging from a rope, how it's tied in place. Instead of trying to take it down, I continue to feel around for the door, my hands padding over the crude cement walls, noticing how sticky they feel—how everything seems so numb and cold.

"Over here," the voice giggles. "If you want to leave, you have to come here." Her voice is coming from over by the sinks.

I move toward it, almost relieved to be going back toward the light. I feel a trickle of something roll off my lip. I move in front of the mirror, my knees shaking with each step. Sprawled across the glass—over my image, the blood trickling down my lips—are giant red letters that say CLARA WAS HERE. Below it is Friday's date—still two days away.

"She *was* here," the voice whispers, "but now she's gone. Because you were too late."

"No," I say, fighting the urge to cover over my ears. "I'm here. She's here. You're *her*."

"Not anymore. She's out on the beach. Haven't you seen her body?"

I turn from the mirror and see her—Clara. Only she looks different than normal—her coloring is grayish and her lips look pale blue. She's wearing a coral-colored sarong with an olive-green T-shirt, and she's carrying a camera—a big and bulky one, like a Polaroid. There's a patch of blood at her middle. It runs down her legs, making a puddle on the floor. She moves into the stall at the end, closing the door and locking it behind her.

I take a step backward, my heel crunching down on something. I look. It's a heart-shaped box. I move to pick it up, recognizing the shiny golden color right away—a one-pound box of Godiva chocolates.

My hands shake. I drop the chocolates to the floor. "Drea?" I whisper, wondering if she's here, if she's the one who left them.

I move back toward the exit door, but it's still too dark to see. I pad along the walls, my heart walloping inside my chest, my hands all jittery. I think I feel a hinge. I follow it around the doorframe, my fingers working their way along the door crack. I feel for the handle, find it, and pull.

It's locked.

I pull harder, try pushing outward, pound at the door with all my might. But it's no use.

I'm trapped.

I move back toward the window, keeping an eye on Clara's bathroom stall. The door is still closed, but it doesn't appear as though she's even in there. I bend down to look for her feet and legs, but it's just empty, like she snuck out. Or maybe she's standing on the toilet. I don't know. I just need to get out of here.

I hoist myself onto the corner sink and stand up, wondering if I'll be able to fit myself through the window. The bottom of my sandal slips against the porcelain; my foot lands in the basin, making me have to grasp the window ledge to keep from falling. I secure my elbows on the ledge and crank the window open, my ankles shaking slightly, like I could topple over at any second. I look back at Clara's stall, but I'm not up quite high enough to see down into it, to see if she's inside.

I take a deep breath and try to refocus. The warm breeze through the window eases me a bit, makes me feel a little less trapped. I continue to crank the lever, but the glass only opens to halfway. "Hello?" I call out.

But instead of the beach, it's just the ocean outside, like the bathroom itself is floating in the middle of the sea. In the distance, I can see someone grappling in the water, trying to stay afloat. I can't see his face, but I know. I can feel it. It's the guy from before—the one carrying the bouquet of lilies. He stops struggling when he sees me, the bouquet of lilies floating up beside him. I feel myself freeze over. I shout out to him and try cranking the window open farther, but it won't budge. And he's starting to sink.

I peer down at Clara's stall, wondering if she can help, but when I look back out the window to check on him, he's already gone.

I take deep breath, my head all dizzy from the rocking of this bathroom, the way the ocean pulls it from side to side. I climb down off the sink, eager to gain a solid footing. There's something on the floor in front of Clara's stall now. A doll. I'm thinking it's the doll that hung in front of the exit door, the one hanging from the rope.

I climb back down, wondering if Clara has left it for me. Blood drips down over the doll's face from my lip. I wipe my nose on my sleeve, noticing how the doll looks just like me—dark hair, light skin, tilty golden-brown eyes. There are pins stuck into the doll's body, like somebody's warped idea of voodoo, like this isn't real—a twisted mirage of some sort.

The bathroom has gone dead quiet now. Even the dripping from the faucets has stopped. I peer up toward the window, wondering if the guy with the lilies is just outside, hoping he won't be able to climb his way in.

I wrap my hand around the doll just as Clara grabs my wrist, stopping me. Her blue-gray hand reaches out from underneath the bathroom stall door. She clenches me hard, pinching my skin. Making me scream.

twenty-six

My scream wakes me up. I'm still in my bed, still in my robe. And the hourglass is still by my night table, all the sand drained down to the bottom. I sit up and close my dream box, confident that the images of my dreams lie inside. A dribble of blood rolls off my upper lip. I grab a wad of toilet paper from the pocket of my robe, thankful that I planned ahead.

I reach under my pillow for my folded piece of paper and press it into my palm, wondering what the truth really is. I close my eyes, conjuring up the images from my night-mare. Clearly the image of Clara was some corpselike version of her—the result of not being able to save her. I picture the blood rolling down her limbs, onto the floor, wondering how or why she's bleeding. Was she stabbed? Did someone cut her? Maybe it has something to do with the doll. But what's weird is that the doll looked just like me, and there were needles sticking right through it—long, pointed pins pierced through the heart. Like maybe I'm the one in danger.

I take a deep breath, thinking about the Polaroid camera. It seems so obvious that it might have something to do with the photographer who lives next door. But is that too obvious? Maybe he's the one with the lilies. Maybe before I find Clara and surgically attach her to my hip, I should pay him another visit.

I glance at the clock. It's a little after three. I change from my robe into a bathing suit, throw on a pair of shorts and a tank top, slip into my flip-flops, and stuff the chunky crystal rock Jacob gave me into my pocket, suddenly remembering the mirror in my dream. I close my eyes and picture the words written in red across it—Clara's name plus Friday's date, which means that I have less than forty-eight hours to figure everything out.

Or else Clara will die.

*　　*　　*

I'm almost out the door when Drea and Amber ambush me. "We seriously need to talk," Drea says.

"Only if you can walk and talk," I say. "I don't have time to waste."

"Where are you going?" Drea asks, following me down the deck stairs.

"To that photographer's place."

"The skeevy guy with the tentacles?" Amber asks.

"The one and only."

"Cool!" Amber exclaims.

"It's not a game," I say.

Drea sighs. "No kidding."

"Why, what's up?"

"We went to the police."

"And?"

"Fish," Amber says. "Big and holy mackerel."

"Excuse me?"

"There's something huge-fishy going on."

"Well, yeah," I say.

"No," Drea says. "They were asking us all these weird questions about Chad."

"Like what?"

"Like, how long he and Clara have known each other; how long me and Chad have been dating; if Chad has a temper; if I think he might be the one doing all this to Clara."

"*What?*" I ask, stopping short.

"Fishy . . ." Amber sings.

"I don't know what she told them," Drea says, "but right now, I'd just like to smash her giggly little face."

"Has Chad gone to the police yet?"

"I don't think so," Drea says. "But I don't know. I haven't seen him anywhere."

"We'll get to the bottom of this," I say, "but right now I have to go."

"I feel horrible, Stacey," Drea continues. "I had to tell them how Chad and I got into a fight, how I caught them all cuddly together."

"I know," I say. "I'm sorry, but at least Chad isn't going to end up dead in less than forty-eight hours."

"We have a T.O.D.?" Amber asks, arching her eyebrows.

"Huh?" Drea and I say in unison.

"Time of death," she says, rolling her eyes like it's obvious.

"Friday," I say. "I dreamt it."

"And you dreamt that it was the photographer guy."

"No," I say, shaking my head. "I mean, I don't know. I'm just going on a hunch."

"Personally, I think we'd be better off going after Casey," Drea says. "We saw him ripping apart his ex earlier—completely yelling at her in front of everybody."

"Why?"

Amber shrugs. "Something about her getting all jealous and possessive of him. She must have seen how soaking he is on me."

"Yeah, right," Drea says, flashing her the okay sign.

"Look," I say. "I don't have time. Are you guys coming with me or not?"

"Wouldn't miss it for all the fortune cookies in China," Amber says, pulling one from her pocket. She cracks it open and reads the fortune aloud: "Life's a stitch and then you sew." She laughs and stuffs both cookie halves into her mouth.

twenty-seven

We climb the stairs of the photographer's cottage and ring the doorbell a couple times, but he doesn't answer. I open the screen door and try knocking. Still no response.

"Maybe he's on a shoot," Drea suggests.

"Shoot my ass," Amber says.

"Seriously?" Drea asks.

"Tell me," Amber says, "why would a photographer for *Vogue* ever want to take pictures of Clara?"

"He obviously has bad taste," Drea says. "I mean, if it *is* him."

Amber takes off her earring, a long and thin sterling silver zigzag. "Cover me," she says, jabbing the point into the lock and maneuvering it around.

"If that doesn't work, I have a credit card," Drea says.

"With you?" I look at her outfit—a tankini top with surfer shorts, no visible pockets anywhere.

"Oh yeah. I never leave home without it."

"Got it," Amber says. The lock clicks, and she turns the knob. "We're so in."

We follow Amber inside, locking the door back up behind us. Just like before, the place is completely dark, the shades all pulled down and no lamps in sight.

"Is he a troll?" Drea asks.

"Maybe Clara lives here." Amber makes a troll of a face, complete with droopy eyes and a tongue that sticks out over her bottom lip.

"Let's go check out the darkroom." I lead them in there and click on the light, feeling that cold, familiar chill run across my shoulders.

The room is set up just like before—the red lightbulb shines down over a clothesline with pictures attached, a workstation full of bins and solutions, and racks that line the walls.

"What are we looking for?" Drea asks.

"Anything that looks suspicious—pictures of Clara, any Polaroids, anything that seems odd."

"Where do we begin?" Amber picks a photo up off the floor. She flashes it to us; it's a picture of a dog taking a whiz on the beach.

"*Vogue,* I think not," Drea says.

"Hey, check it out." Amber plucks a photo from the clothesline. "I think I recognize this girl. I think she works at the Clam Stripper."

Drea and I join her to look. It's a picture of some girl wearing a short sundress on the beach.

"Oh my god," Drea says, her gaze wandering down the line. The clothesline is full of snapshots of girls—unsuspecting females on the beach, swimming in the water, and rubbing suntan oil onto their legs.

"What a perv!" Amber bellows.

Drea has already made her way down the end of the clothesline. "Oh my god," she says. "There's some of me. And this one's of Stacey."

Amber and I join her to scavenge through the clothesline of photos. There's got to be at least two hundred pictures here and twenty-two of them are of us—Drea, playing in the water with Chad, cuddling up beside him, and rubbing suntan oil over her stomach and legs; Amber, patting some guy's dog and playing beached whale; and me, sitting at the shoreline with Jacob and wading in the water. There's also a handful of Clara: Clara at the Clam Stripper, Clara tanning on the beach, Clara with an ice cream cone. The thing is there's nothing unique or unusual about them—they're just like all the rest.

"I feel so dirty," Drea says, covering her mouth. "Look at this one—you can see my tan lines." Drea points to the strip of white across her back upper thigh.

"With an angle like that," Amber says, eyeing the picture, "I'd say the tan line is the least of your problems."

"These are just like the pictures left in Clara's room," I say, interrupting them, ". . . the ones in the envelope."

"Don't compare *us* to *her*," Drea snaps.

I take a deep breath, holding myself back from bopping her head off. "All I'm saying is that those pictures were candid—like these. She had no idea she was even being photographed."

"Right," Amber says, "which brings us back to my perv theory."

"I don't think it's him," I say.

"Are you blind?" Drea asks, gesturing toward the clothes-line of photos.

"If it was him, then he'd have way more pictures of Clara than just three. He'd have a whole shrine dedicated to her."

"Let's not forget about the whole envelope of Clara shots left in her room," Drea says.

"Exactly," I say. "Someone who takes that many peeping-Tom pictures of one individual—while she's in her cottage, changing her clothes, and getting ready for a shower . . . you'd think he'd have kept a bunch for himself. I mean, if he's that obsessed with her . . ."

"Maybe he does have a bunch," Amber says. "Maybe they're just hidden somewhere."

"So let's get to it," I say.

While Drea collects the photos of us into a stack and searches around for more, Amber announces that she's off to snoop through his medicine cabinet and "bedroom good-ies." Meanwhile, I resume rifling through the darkroom. I dig my way through camera equipment, development chemicals, and photos of all genres, from apples to zebras—quiet literally.

"This is useless," I hear Amber shout from the other room. "No Polaroids, no more pictures of Clara, no dead bodies in the closet."

"She's right," Drea says, itching at her sides. "Let's get out of here. I feel all skeevy."

At that moment the back door shuts, like someone just came in.

"Oh my god," Drea mouths. She stuffs the photos of us up the back of her tankini.

"Wait here," Amber whispers. She tiptoes toward the doorway and peers down the hallway. "In the kitchen," she mouths, hearing the tinkling of a dish. "Come on."

"No way," Drea mouths.

"Now," Amber whispers. She takes a right down the hallway, heading for the front door. I follow, grabbing Drea by the arm as I exit the room. The floorboards creak beneath our steps. My heart quickens; my stomach churns. I hear more noise in the kitchen, like the slamming of a microwave door. Meanwhile, Amber's fingers are working the front lock. She turns it—click.

"Hey there," he says.

We all freeze. I grit my teeth and turn to look. He isn't there. I look back at Amber, her eyes wide and expectant.

More noises continue in the kitchen—utensils against a plate, maybe, the sound of a carbonated drink bubbling over. "Yup. Just got back," his voice continues.

"He's on the phone," Amber mouths. She turns back to the door, opens it wide for all of us to exit. And we're out. We're free.

twenty-eight

After getting a relatively safe distance away, we slow our pace to a brisk walk, not even realizing that we've already passed our cottage.

"Wait," Drea says. "Where are we going?"

I shake my head, my heart still pounding. "That was just a little too close."

"But we made it," Amber says.

"Because of luck," Drea gasps. "Because the guy got hungry and he needed to call somebody."

"Maybe," I say.

"What are you guys talking about?" Amber asks. "We made it out of sheer talent."

"I don't know," I say, leading us back in the direction of the cottage. "Maybe he wasn't really on the phone. Maybe he just wanted us to think he was."

"And why would he ever do that?" Amber asks.

"I don't know. It just seemed a little too easy."

"Easy or not," Drea says, repeatedly wiping her palms on her surfer shorts, "I couldn't be happier to be out of that creep's place. I think I need to bathe for at least an hour." Drea grabs the photos of us from the back of her tankini. "I mean, what do you think he does with all these pictures?"

"What do I think he does *with* them or in front of them?" Amber snatches the photos from Drea and begins flipping through them.

"Nix the bath," Drea says. "I need to stand in a *car wash* for the next six hours."

"Fine," I say. "You disinfect, I'll think, and then we'll decide our next move. But first, let me feel the photos." I go to take them from Amber.

"Sick," Amber says, stepping away.

"You *know* what I mean. I want to feel them for vibrations."

"There are much easier ways to vibrate," she says, handing the photos over anyway.

I run my fingers over the surfaces.

"Well?" Drea asks.

I concentrate harder, closing my eyes and running my fingers over each one. "Skeevy," I say.

"No kidding." Drea shudders.

"Major skeeviness, like he knew that taking pictures of us was wrong, but it's like it didn't matter."

"Um, yeah," Amber says, "because he's a psycho-perv. Doesn't take a genius to figure it out."

"Which is why you were able to," Drea says to her.

"It's weird, though," I say, ignoring their banter. "The pictures of Clara, the Polaroid ones left in her bedroom, they felt different—cold, like death."

"What about those photo-duds we found on the floor?" Amber asks. "The maybe-an-arm and could-be-a-butt-cheek snapshots? Did you happen to feel those?"

I shake my head. "I picked them up, but Clara took them right away. She thinks that someone planted them there."

"What do you mean?" Drea asks.

"She thought it was too weird that someone would fill an entire envelope full of photos and then just drop a couple in their path."

"That's actually not a bad point," Amber says. "Even for a skank. But why would someone plant them? You couldn't even tell what they were."

I shrug. "I don't know. It doesn't make sense."

"What I don't get," Drea says, "is if it's the skeevy photographer who's doing all this, why did he use a Polaroid camera for some photos but not all? The only Polaroids we found were the ones left in her bedroom."

"Right," I say. "So maybe it isn't him."

"Or maybe he is," Amber says. "If I were gonna take crazy stalker photos of someone, that's what I'd use. It's way too risky to take the film to be developed someplace."

"Brilliant, Einstein," Drea says, "but he obviously develops his own film. Was the creepy darkroom not a big enough tip-off for you?"

Amber middle-finger scratches the side of her nose in reply.

"You know she's planning on going on the fundraiser cruise tomorrow," Drea says.

I nod. "Which means that I'll have to go, too."

"We'll *all* be going," Drea corrects. She reaches out to touch my forearm, reminding me that I'm not alone in this.

We climb the deck steps of our cottage, swing the door open, and sitting on the couch is Clara, but she's not alone.

Clara's limbs are entangled with Chad's. She's lying on top of him, her mouth suctioned against his. I go to jump in front of Drea, to pull her back outside so she won't see, but it's too late. Her mouth drops open at the picture of it—of them.

Clara peeps an eye open and sees us. "Oh, wow!" she yelps.

Chad jumps up, and I feel myself reach out to Drea. I clasp her forearm and can feel her trembling. Clara fumbles to sit up, covering the slit in her sarong, pulling at her T-shirt for proper placement.

"Drea," Chad says, standing up. "It was an accident."

"What? Did her lips fall on you by mistake?"

"Actually, that can happen," Amber says.

"I hate you!" Drea shouts at them, though I'm not sure who she's talking to, if it's Clara or Chad. "Don't talk to me. Don't try and make it up to me. And save me the insult of trying to explain it all away."

"You don't understand," he pleas. "It was a mistake. Things just got out of hand."

"He's right," Clara says. "I came here because I was upset. Chad was just trying to comfort me."

"I could use a little of that kind of comforting," Amber whispers.

I elbow her in response.

"I got more threats," Clara continues. "Someone wants to kill me."

"Well, he'll have to wait in line," Drea snaps.

A part of me wants to ask Clara about it, but I'm too concerned about Drea right now.

"Can we talk about this?" Chad asks her.

"I have nothing to say to you." Drea takes one last look at him before taking off into the bathroom and slamming the door shut behind her.

twenty-nine

Instead of trying to make amends with Drea, Chad holes himself up in the guys' room, slamming the door shut behind him. I tell Clara to leave, that I'll call her later, and then Amber and I head into the bathroom to check on Drea. Despite her funk and fuming, she tells us that we should head over to the frat house to reserve our spots on the cruise ship tomorrow night.

"Don't even worry about that right now," I tell her.

"You *have* to worry about it," Drea says, balling up a tissue to wipe at her nose. "I heard Sully mention yesterday that the cruise was filling up. I need to be on it. I need to get away from Chad."

"How can you even think about the cruise?" Amber asks. "Five minutes ago that skank was lip-suctioned to your man. That boy's gonna need some serious tetanus."

Drea smiles slightly in response, but then her lips turn downward again. "Maybe there will be some cuter boys on the cruise—way cuter than Chad. Maybe I'll hook up with one of them. How will he like that?"

"Yes!" Amber cheers. "Jealousy is the sweetest revenge."

"It might be sweet," I say, "but it isn't smart."

Amber rolls her eyes in response. "Leave it to Stacey Straight Lace to pee on our plans."

"I really just want to be alone right now," Drea says, pausing me from firing back at Amber.

"No way," I say, presenting Drea with a fresh box of tissues from the bathroom closet. "You need us."

"What I need is a long, hot bath with sea salts, my gel-filled eye mask, and lots of chocolate."

"Are you sure?"

She nods. "I'll be okay."

"So I take it we're *not* getting tickets for the guys," Amber says.

A good question, but I don't answer.

"I think we should let them sink," Amber says.

"I second that." Drea sniffles.

"This should totally be a girls' night thing," Amber continues.

"It's not exactly going to be fun," I remind her. "We *do* have Clara to worry about." I glance up at Drea, almost regretting the mere mentioning of Clara's name.

"Don't remind me," Drea says, grabbing another tissue to wipe her runny mascara.

"Yeah, but not until Friday," Amber corrects. "That means we have all night Thursday to party it up."

I sigh my frustration, not wanting to get into it with her—how little I feel like partying, how I'd give anything right now not to have Clara's future sitting on my shoulders.

Before leaving, Amber and I set Drea up with bath salts, her freshly chilled gel mask (pulled straight from the fridge), some of my favorite bath oils (chamomile and rose), and a box of chocolate-walnut fudge Amber bought at the candy shop downtown.

We climb the porch steps to frat-boy central, the smell of stale beer mixed with sweat already thick in the air. Sully greets us at the door. "What's up?" he asks.

But we're still arguing over how many tickets to buy.

"Hold up," he says, interrupting us. "Your guys already bought your tickets."

"Huh?" we say in unison.

"Yeah, I'm pretty sure. Hold on." He goes back inside, retrieving a clipboard from the kitchen table. He flips through several pages before finding our reservation. He nods, reading through all our names—all of us except Jacob.

"They're *so* sweet," Amber says.

"Wait," I say. "What about Jacob?"

"The quiet guy?"

I nod. "With the dark hair."

"Yeah," Sully says. "He said something about not being able to make it."

"Why can't he make it?" I snap.

"Hey, don't kill the messenger."

Amber wraps her arm around my shoulder. "At least he bought *your* ticket."

"So we'll see you tomorrow night," Sully says.

"Wait," Amber says. "How many rooms did the guys reserve?"

Sully checks his clipboard. "Two."

I nod, still confused about Jacob. Though with everything that's been happening between us, I'm not even sure why.

"Should be a good time," Sully says.

Amber takes a pause to openly ogle him up and down. "You can count on it." We walk back to our cottage in silence, Amber's arm still wrapped around my shoulder for support.

"One of us should check on Drea," I say, once inside.

"I'll go," Amber says. "You have enough on your plate right now. Go fix things with your man."

"Kind of hard to fix things when he's never around."

Amber responds by knocking on the guys' room door. "What?" Chad hollers from inside.

"Is Jacob in there?"

"Nope."

Amber's lips bunch up in disapproval. But she couldn't be more disappointed than I am.

"I told you," I say.

Amber sighs. "Maybe Drea still has some chocolate left—I think *I* could use some right about now." While she heads off to check on Drea and rob her of her edible vices, I distract myself with work by giving Clara a call.

"Hello?" she answers.

"Hi, it's Stacey. I just wanted to see how you're doing."

"I've been better."

"So has Drea," I say. A direct stinger.

Clara doesn't respond.

After several seconds, I break the silence. "You said something before about getting more threats. . . . What happened?"

"We can talk about it later," she says. "I'm going to a barbecue with my parents. . . . It's at some friends of theirs. I should actually get going."

"When will you be back?"

"I don't know. I think it might be late. I can call you tomorrow."

I hesitate a moment, but then remind myself that we still have more than twenty-four hours. "You'll be with your parents all night?"

"Who else?" she says. "It's not like they're letting me out of their sight for more than five minutes."

"Okay," I say, biting at my bottom lip. "Then I'll see you first thing tomorrow. We have a lot to talk about."

"I agree," she says. But there's something about the way she says it.

Like she has an agenda of her own.

thirty

I decide to end my day with a long walk on the beach, capped off with a much-needed meditation session. The outgoing tide helps to center me; it helps me imagine all the negative energy swimming out to sea. When I get back to the cottage, I continue my blissful breather by turning in early. Drea has followed suit. She's camped herself out in bed with a stack of *Teen* magazines, a box of chocolates, and her diary. Part of me wants to tell her what happened with Jacob and the tickets, but I feel like that would be almost selfish of me, adding the weight of my relationship stress to hers. Plus, it's Jacob I should really be confronting.

I look at the clock. It's just after nine. I know Jacob will probably come walking through the outside door any second now, that he'll probably want to see me. But maybe I'm sick of being so accessible to him. Maybe he's the one who should have to wait.

"How are you doing?" I ask, pulling the bed sheet up to my waist.

"I'm doing," she says, continuing to scribble away in her diary, probably massacring Chad in cold, hard ink.

"Do you want to talk about it?"

"He thinks he can fix all his screw-ups with chocolate. This is the third box in two weeks."

"Why not hint at flowers next time? They're much easier on the teeth."

"Not to mention the waistline." Drea holds the heart-shaped box out to me as an offering.

That's when I notice. It's the same box of chocolates I saw in my last nightmare about Clara. I clench my teeth and shake my head, wondering if she should even be eating them, assuring myself that they're from Chad, that he would never hurt her.

"Good night," she says, clicking off her lamp.

I click off my lamp as well and slide down into the bliss of cool cotton sheets, telling myself that it's just a random case of déjà-vu.

The next morning, I'm the first person up. It's 10:30, which completely surprises me since my body isn't chemically wired to sleep in past nine. I slip into my fuzzy slippers, realizing that I don't remember what I dreamt last night—or if I dreamt at all. I look over at my dream box, positioned on my night table with the lid closed. So maybe my body's just telling me that I needed some extra rest, which is probably why my nose is still dry, why I'm not scrambling for a tissue.

I move into the kitchen to percolate some coffee, grab a box of Rice Krispies, and sit down at the table to enjoy the sound of solitude. Of course, no sooner do my Krispies start snap-crackle-popping than my solitude turns into an ice storm. Drea and Chad exit their rooms at practically the same time. Drea evil-eyes Chad before going into the bathroom, caddy of bathing products in tow, and slamming the door shut behind her.

"She hates me," Chad says, grabbing a box of powdered donuts from the top of the fridge.

Amber joins us a few seconds later, still yawning as she plunks herself down at the table. "What's for breakfast?"

I slide the box of Krispies her way.

"No way." She gets up, fishes through the cabinets for jars of peanut butter and jam, and then grabs a spoon to dig in like pudding. "So what are we talking about?" she asks, propping her frog-slippered feet up on the table.

"Drea hates me," Chad repeats.

"I wonder why." Amber purposefully licks her spoon.

"It wasn't my fault," he says. "Clara totally went after me."

"And your lips just happened to lose the fight?" Amber rolls her eyes. "How many times have I heard *that* excuse before?"

"She was upset," he continues, "about some doll that was left in her room."

"A doll?" I say, snapping to attention.

"Yeah, some whacked-up doll with pins stuck through the heart. She was convinced the doll was supposed to look like her."

"How did it get in her room if her parents are home?" I ask.

"I don't know. I guess her bedroom window was left open or something like that. The girl doesn't think."

"Which is why she kissed *you*," Amber says.

Chad ignores Amber to continue his groveling at me. "I was trying to calm her down, you know. But I could tell she had another agenda."

"And jamming her tongue down your throat was the first item on it?" Amber asks. "She really *doesn't* think."

"I'm serious," he continues. "She kept staring at my mouth and getting closer until she was practically sitting in my lap."

"So why didn't you just get up?" I ask him.

"I don't know; I didn't want to be rude."

"Wow," Amber gasps. "That would have to be the worst excuse *ever*."

He sighs and runs his fingers through his hair. "I know. I messed up."

"Big time." I push my cereal bowl away and glance back up at the clock, thinking how I should probably go ask Clara about the doll, how I probably won't have much alone time with her later since we'll be on that stupid cruise amidst a hundred drunken frat boys. "I should go check on Clara."

"Do you want me to come?" Amber asks.

I shake my head, hoping that Clara might confide more if we're alone.

"Good luck to you," Chad says, with a raise of the eyebrows.

"You're the one who needs luck," Amber says to him. "You think you're in trouble with the police? Wait till Drea gets through with you."

"What are you talking about? Why am I in trouble with the police?"

"Haven't you heard? When Drea and I talked to the police yesterday, they were extra quizzy about you."

"Why?"

Amber shrugs. "They made it seem like you're a suspect."

"*Me?*"

She nods. "It almost seemed like they thought you and Clara have something scandalous going."

"Are you kidding me?" His eyes are completely bulging now.

"Imagine that," she says, licking the spoon again.

"You should probably go and talk to the police," I tell him. "Set them straight. Maybe Clara got the wrong idea about something."

"How?"

"*How?*" Amber gasps. "Are you for real?"

"Just tell the police the truth," I say. "You have nothing to hide."

"Are you kidding?" he says. "I know that drill. I go talk to them; they start asking all these tricky questions; the next thing I know I'm their number-one suspect."

I can understand his reluctance, to a point. When Drea was being stalked junior year, Chad, after agreeing to tell the police his side of the story, ended up as one of the police's prime suspects. "I still think you should go and talk to them. I mean, if you don't have anything to hide."

"I don't know," he says. "Maybe I *should* have something to hide. Maybe they'll twist this whole thing into something it isn't. That's obviously what Clara's done."

"I have to go," I say, looking toward the guys' room door. "Is Jacob still in bed?"

"Yup." Chad grins. "You had him up pretty late last night."

"What are you talking about?"

"He didn't get in till after three."

"He didn't?"

Chad's face falls, realizing maybe that he just screwed up. "Oh," he says. "Forget I said anything. I was probably just dreaming."

"Thanks a lot." I bite down hard on my teeth and turn on my heel, suddenly realizing perhaps who my real friends are, suddenly more than anxious to lose myself in someone else's problems.

thirty-one

I head over to Clara's cottage. It's completely sweltering outside, the sun beating down on the crown of my head, sending trickles of sweat along the back of my neck and between my shoulder blades.

I climb the steps and ring the doorbell, the sound of her bamboo wind chimes, bonging just behind me, making my head ache. Several seconds pass—still no one has come to the door. I move to peer over the side of the deck, toward the driveway, but I don't see a car either. Did she go out again with her parents?

I knock. Still no response. I try the door and, this time, it's locked. Perfect. I walk around to the front of the cottage. There's a car parked out front; the license plate says New York, even though I could have sworn Clara said she was from Connecticut. Still, the back is packed up with luggage, so I'm assuming it's her parents' car, back from their friend's place, finally. I begin toward the steps, but the trashcans catch my eye. Amber's always talking about how on cop shows they find the good clues by sifting through the trash.

The two aluminum cans are sitting on the curb between Clara's neighbor's cottage and hers. I study the sides, looking for a last name or number to indicate whom they belong to, but only find dents. I casually glance around to see if anybody's looking and lift one of the lids. Sheer grossness—spaghetti mixed with soggy paper towels and coffee grounds. I try the other lid—paper goods, quite doable. I pick through coupon flyers, old newspaper ads, and a bunch of chocolate-bar wrappers until I get to the bottom.

There's a small can of paint sitting there. It's tipped onto its side, the bright cherry redness spilling onto a wad of orange peels. I look closer, noting how there's a smudge of red on the cap as well, wondering if it's the same shade as the paint used to graffiti Clara's bedroom wall.

So who threw it away here? I look to her neighbor's house, wondering who lives there, if these trashcans belong to them. Or maybe whoever graffitied Clara's walls threw it away on their way out—to get rid of the evidence. But that doesn't make sense either. Why would someone choose to throw away evidence at the scene of the crime?

Instead of trying to figure it all out right here and now, I reach in, grab the paint can, and make my way up Clara's front steps. I ring the doorbell once more just to be sure there's still no one home—there isn't—and try the doorknob. It turns. "Hello?" I call, edging the door open. "Clara?"

There are a couple suitcases lined up in the entryway, but it doesn't appear as though anyone's home. So why, then, do I feel like I'm not alone?

I move slowly down the hallway toward Clara's room, noticing how her bedroom door is open a crack. "Clara?" I call, before going in. The graffiti is still there on the wall. I go to compare it with the can of paint, but the sight of the doll makes me jump.

It's in her bed, tucked beneath the covers—rosy-cheeked with auburn hair and sea glass-green eyes. Just like Clara. A shiver runs down my back. I look over my shoulder toward the door, wondering if I'm alone.

Or if someone might be watching me.

I pick the doll up, noticing right away the pins stuck through the belly. I run my fingers along the back, trying to sense something, accidentally pricking my finger with one of the pins. With a gasp I drop the doll, my heart strumming hard inside my chest. I poke my thumb into my mouth to stop the bleeding. It's a tiny puncture wound, like the kind you get at the doctor's. I pick the doll up once more and concentrate on the eyes, the way they fall closed when she's positioned vertically—like she's dead.

I peek once again over my shoulder and then continue to feel the rubbery skin. I glide my fingers up the arms, along the neck, and over the cheeks, but all I can sense is sadness—a sadness so thick and heavy I can feel it in my lungs, making my breath heavy.

The sound of running water starts from behind the wall. I look up, suddenly realizing that what I thought was Clara's closet door must really be the door to her adjoining bathroom.

"Clara?" I call. I move around the bed to the door and place my ear up against the panel to listen. The water falls down in a heavy stream, like it's coming from a tub faucet. I knock and hear a shuffling inside, like someone's struggling to put stuff away. "Clara?"

I go to turn the knob. At the same moment, the door pulls open, causing both of us to jump. Clara stumbles back, and I drop the doll once again.

"What are you doing here?" she asks, pushing her hair back off her face. She looks a mess. Her eyes are raw, like she's been crying, and there are dark circles beneath them.

"Are you okay?"

"Yeah." She tries to fake a smile, but it just falls flat. "You scared me. How did you get in?"

"The front door was open. I tried to knock, but no one answered. Didn't you hear—"

"What's that?" she shrieks, referring to the paint can. She looks up at the graffiti and takes a step away, as though to close the door on me.

"No, Clara—wait. I found this in the trash outside. Who lives next door to you?"

"Huh?"

"Are those your trashcans out front?"

Her face twists up. "Yeah."

"Well, then, I think whoever painted the graffiti on your wall threw the paint can in the trash on their way out. We need to take it to the police. Maybe they can use it as evidence."

"I gotta go," she says, taking another step back.

"Look, Clara," I say. "I'm sorry I scared you, but you have to believe me." I take a deep breath, thinking how unbelievably unconvincing I must sound to her—after having broken into her house not once but *twice* now.

She nods and studies me, the rims of her eyes extra puffy and red.

"We're on the same team here," I continue.

"Are you sure about that?"

"Why wouldn't I be?"

She shrugs and looks away. "Because of what happened yesterday . . . with Chad."

My hands clench into fists just thinking about how hurt Drea was—how hurt she still is. "I still need to help you."

"You weren't there, Stacey," she says. "You don't know how it happened."

"I was there long enough."

"We didn't plan for it to happen . . . it just did."

I close my eyes in an effort to block out the mental images of Clara and Chad lip-locked.

"He really cares about me," she continues. "And I care about him, too."

"He *has* a girlfriend."

"That didn't stop *you*. He told me how you went after him two years ago even though he and Drea were still kind of together."

My mouth drops open. "That's not true."

"How else would I know?"

I bite the inside of my cheek to keep from exploding. "That isn't how it happened, but it doesn't even matter. You're in danger, and we need to talk about it."

"Who cares? It's not like everybody I meet doesn't end up hating me after five minutes."

"You're exaggerating," I say, stretching the truth out like taffy. I peer past her into the bathroom—a stark white cube with matching porcelain fixtures and terrycloth towels. "Your tub water's still running."

She shrugs and then nods, as though just remembering. "He moved some of my stuff around again—the guy who's doing all this." She glances over her shoulder at the letter opener positioned on the vanity. "I know I put it back in my desk."

"He?" I ask.

She shrugs. "I think so. He left me something, too." She moves to her night table and opens the drawer, taking out a shiny gold heart-shaped box of chocolates. "I found it first thing this morning, wedged into my window, between the screen and the sill. Weird," she says, glancing at the window. "I could have sworn I locked it."

"Clara—" I say, my eyes widening, my heart pumping hard.

"What?"

But I have no idea what to say. I mean, why would Clara get the same box of chocolates that Chad gave Drea? Is it a mere coincidence? Is someone trying to make it look like Chad's doing all this? Or did Chad maybe leave the box for Clara because he was feeling guilty about yesterday?

"Was there a note?"

She nods and hands it to me—a plain white card that says "To Clara. Love, Me."

I look at her, my face crinkling up in confusion. "This doesn't make sense."

She shakes her head. "None of it does."

"No, I mean, it *really* doesn't make sense. Why would someone write hateful graffiti on your wall one day and then leave you chocolates and a love note the next?"

Clara shrugs, snatching the note back and returning it and the box of chocolates into the night table drawer. "Who knows? Maybe they're not from the same person."

"Is there something you want to tell me?"

"No, but maybe there's something *you* can tell *me.* What happened between Drea and that boy who was supposedly stalking her a couple years ago?"

"Donovan?"

She nods.

"He was obsessed with her. He had been since the third grade. The obsession got out of hand; he thought there was more to their relationship. There wasn't. He couldn't handle it."

"And you think he was going to kill her?"

"Are you in a similar situation?" I ask, ignoring the question.

"I don't know. I mean, it really sounds like Donovan loved Drea. I'm not sure this guy feels the same way about me. Sometimes I kind of wish he did."

"Clara," I say, "you don't know what you're talking about."

"Maybe *you* don't."

I hold back my gasp and silently count to ten, reminding myself that Clara is obviously starved for attention. "Where are your parents?"

"The Clam Stripper. Then we're all supposed to be taking a ride to some all-day art show. I was actually supposed to join them for lunch after my bath." Clara lifts her arm, like she's going to check the time, but she's not wearing a watch. Instead, there's a deep, blood-filled scratch down her forearm.

"What happened?" I touch Clara's arm, and she jerks away.

"The doll," she says. "It was in my bed. I rolled over on it."

"What do you think the doll means?"

"What do *you* think? It's obviously me. He obviously wants to kill me."

"Why?"

She shrugs. "Maybe I messed things up for him."

"*Things?* As in relationship things?"

"I can't really talk right now," she whispers, as though there's someone else in the room.

"Wait," I say. "Are you talking about Chad?"

"I should get going. My parents are really freaked about this whole thing. They almost weren't gonna let me go on the cruise."

"Clara . . ."

"Just don't tell anyone about all this."

My heart squelches just hearing these words—the words from my nightmares. "About what?" I ask, swallowing hard.

"About everything. I'm beginning to think too many people know my business."

"Like who?"

Instead of answering, Clara moves back into the bathroom doorway. She purses her lips and looks away. "If you tell, I'll know, Stacey."

My skin chills over. "And then you'll make me pay?"

She looks back at me, her face twisted up into a giant question mark. "What are you talking about?"

"Forget it."

"I gotta go," she says.

"Clara, we need to talk." I hold the door wide to keep her from shutting it on me.

"Later, okay? My parents will have a fit if I don't get going."

I bite my bottom lip, feeling a sudden urgency to go and talk to Chad, to get to the bottom of whatever's going on between them. Plus, I remind myself, my nightmares tell me that she isn't in danger until tomorrow, leaving us tonight to figure things out. "Let's get together later," I say. "After your art show."

"After the art show I'll be on the cruise."

"Fine. I'll see you then."

She nods and I leave, hoping I haven't made a huge mistake by letting her off so easily.

thirty-two

I barge into our cottage, eager to talk to Chad. He's sitting at the kitchen table, paging through a magazine and devouring a can of sour cream and onion Pringles. "Hey," he says, as soon as I come in. He flips the magazine closed to focus on me. "Did you talk to Clara?"

"Oh, I talked to her all right," I say, wondering where I should even begin.

"And?"

"Where's Drea?" I look toward the bathroom door, knowing full well that she's not prepared to hear what I have to say.

"She went out with PJ and Amber. I wasn't exactly invited." No surprise there. "So," he continues. "What happened?" His face is completely serious, his eyes wide like he knows something's up.

I fold my arms across my chest. "I think Clara might be under the impression that you guys have something serious brewing."

"*Serious?*"

"Yeah, you know, something claddagh-ring worthy."

"Nothing happened between us. Well, nothing *serious,*" he corrects.

"Did you leave chocolates in her window, outside her bedroom?"

"Huh?"

"She said someone left her a box of chocolates, tagged 'To Clara. Love, Me.' Apparently she found it first thing this morning."

"That's crazy," Chad says. "Why would I ever—"

"It was the same heart-shaped box you gave Drea."

"*What?*" Chad stands up from the table, the color draining from his face.

I nod. "It's true."

"So what does that mean?" he asks. "You think I left it for her? You think I'd be that stupid?"

"Honestly, I don't know what to think. I just know that none of this makes sense."

"It's a coincidence," he exclaims.

"What is?"

"That she got the same box of chocolates. The candy shop downtown had a huge display of the box I bought."

"Maybe," I say, even though I don't believe in coincidence. "Or maybe somebody's trying to frame you. Did you happen to notice if anyone was watching you at the candy shop?"

"Watching me?"

"Yeah, you know, did anything weird happen? Was anyone following you?"

"I don't know." He sighs. "I picked up the box, went to the register, paid, and then left."

"And that's it? Nothing weird?"

"No." He shrugs. "You have to believe me, Stacey. Nothing's going on between me and her."

"Your perception of it doesn't matter. Clara *thinks* something's going on, and I'm pretty sure she's convinced herself that you feel the same way. That's obviously what she's told the police."

"She thinks it's me who's doing all this, doesn't she?"

"I don't know. I don't think so. But I'd be ready if I were you. The police already asked Amber and Drea if you have a temper."

"This is crazy," Chad says, combing his hands through his hair in frustration. "What would my motive be for stalking Clara? I mean, come on."

I shake my head. "Who knows what else she's told the police? I don't exactly trust her perception of things."

"But you believe me, right? You know I wouldn't do that." I open my mouth to say something, to ease him a bit, but Chad doesn't even give me a chance. "I'm getting a lawyer," he says. "I'm not gonna have this pinned on me."

"You need to relax," I say. "Nothing's happened yet."

"*Yet,*" he repeats, his jaw locking into place.

"Can I just ask one thing?"

"Anything."

"How come you told Clara I went after you while you and Drea were dating? You know that's not how it happened."

"Is that what she said?"

I nod.

"Well, she's lying. I never said that."

"You never said we dated?"

"Well, yeah, I might have told her that—"

"Whatever," I say, completely spent from trying to decode everybody's conversations, from splitting hairs over words. "Is Jacob around?"

Chad gestures to the guys' room. I peek in that direction, but the door is closed. I take a deep breath and move down the hallway toward his room.

"Stacey—wait," Chad calls.

But I'm tired of waiting. I knock on the guys' door. Jacob opens it. "I was wondering where you were," he says. "I thought we might spend the day together."

"Why's that? Because you're skipping the cruise tonight?"

His eyebrows furrow. "What do you mean?"

"The cruise is tonight. Thanks for the ticket, by the way."

"Oh yeah," he says, frowning. "I was going to talk to you about that. Do you think there's any way you can convince Clara not to go?"

"A ship full of guys, a night away from her parents—what do *you* think?"

He sighs. "It's just . . . this cruise . . . I can't do it, Stacey."

"I have a day to figure out who's trying to kill the girl, Jacob. I could really use a little support here."

"I'm sorry," he says quietly.

"You're *sorry*? That's it?"

He looks away, and I feel my teeth clench.

"Don't be angry at me," he whispers. "I want you to go; that's why I bought you a ticket."

I shake my head, a mix of anger and disappointment building up inside my chest. I look away to hide what I'm feeling. "I just thought you might want to be there for me. I guess I was wrong." I turn to walk away, expecting him to stop me.

He doesn't.

thirty-three

I spend the remainder of the day trying my best to relax before the cruise, to not let Jacob's secrets and selfishness get
the better of me, since there's so much at stake right now. I
swim, I lay in the sand, I drink bottled water and snack on
comfort food—peanut-butter-filled pretzels (for the salt)
and gummy worms (for the sugar). It's somewhat thera-
peutic. The warmth of the sun soaking into my skin, coupled with the scrumptiousness of the cool saltwater as I

backstroke through waves, helps lift a bit of the negative energy.

But I still feel confused. I mean, if the situation were reversed, I know I'd be there for Jacob 110 percent. So why won't he be there for me?

When I get back to the cottage, much to my unsurprise, he isn't around. I sigh and drop my beach bag to the ground, noticing PJ. He looks even more depressed than my pre-beach-bum state. He's sitting in the living room, slouched against the wall.

"Are you okay?" I ask him.

"Jim freakin' dandy," he says, yanking at the lime-green gum in his mouth.

"Where's Amber and Drea?"

He shrugs. "Beats the wanky out of me."

"What's wrong with you?"

"What *isn't* wrong?"

"Good point," I joke. But he doesn't laugh. "Seriously," I say. "What's up?"

He proceeds to give me the lowdown on his funkdom—how he messed things up with Amber by thinking he had a chance with Clara, how he messed things up with Clara by not being as "jock-boy-gigolo" as Chad.

"Girls don't like gigolo," I say. "Trust me."

"Are you kidding me?" He stretches his gum out even farther to loop it into a knot. "Girls don't know real charm when they see it."

Despite several attempts to cheer PJ up, including his medicinal pickle-mayo concoction and the *Full House* marathon, PJ remains as deflated as Amber's Superman

blow-up doll, which apparently sprung a leak last night—
he's now slouched at the foot of Amber's bed. PJ is not,
however, depressed enough to cancel his cruising plans. So,
while he goes off to pack for the cruise, I decide that I
should probably start getting ready myself.

I throw some spell staples into a bag, as well as a change
of clothes and some other necessities, and then peer over at
the crystal cluster rock on my night table. I pick it up,
knowing that I'm going to bring it, but wishing more than
anything that Jacob himself were coming with me.

A few seconds later, Amber and Drea come in. Apparently they spent the day checking out all the little boutiques
downtown, as evidenced by the armfuls of shopping bags
they're toting.

"We need to boog," Amber says, checking the clock.
"We board in less than an hour."

"I don't even feel like going anymore," Drea says.

"Tell me about it." I sigh.

"It's a big boat," Amber says. She extracts a bottle of Mr.
Bubble from one of her bags and holds it out to Drea as
though it's supposed to make her feel better. "With any
luck you won't even *see* Chad. You'll be too busy fighting
off all the frat-boy cuties with me."

Drea appears less than convinced. She shrugs and sits
down on the edge of her bed, stuffing her overnight bag
with a handful of nail polish bottles and Chad's box of apology chocolates—telltale signs that it's going to be a long
night. Part of me wants to tell her and Amber that the same
gift appeared on Clara's windowsill, but I decide against it.
It's not that I'm trying to protect Chad, but considering

Drea's state, coupled with the fact that I'm not 100-percent convinced that he's one who left the chocolates in Clara's window, I see no benefit in adding to Drea's angst right now.

By 6:30, Jacob has taken off once again, and Chad and PJ are waiting for Amber, Drea, and me in the living room. So I'm stalling, telling everyone I need to check something in my room, on the back porch, in the newspaper before we go, asking if they can give me just a couple more minutes so I can dash into the bathroom.

It's because I'm waiting—hoping—for Jacob to come back to the cottage. Despite the mess we're in, I just want to say goodbye. I think everyone knows this, which is why they're accommodating my absurd requests.

"We have to go," Chad says finally. "If we don't leave now, we'll miss the boat."

"Literally," Amber says.

I nod, since I know they're right—since I know in my heart that if Jacob wanted to be here for me, then he would be. He'd be piling into Amber's vintage Volkswagen van along with the rest of us, picking through her Wendy's wrappers to find a clean spot to sit, and heading down to the dock.

Just a few minutes away, Amber screeches the van into the parking lot of the docking station, but luckily it seems like we still have time to spare. There's a bunch of people hanging around outside, negotiating over last minute tickets and room selection.

We head up a long and rickety ramp that leads us to the boat. At least one full section of the thick iron railing that encircles the main deck has been removed to allow all us passengers to file aboard. It seems Drea has decided to stick extra close to Amber and me so she doesn't have to talk to Chad. Meanwhile, PJ tries his hardest to work his way back onto Amber's good side. He offers three times to carry her bags before she finally caves and lets him. He also informs her that if she wants to borrow his sunglasses, his sun block, or his squirt gun, then all she has to do is say the word.

The boat is huge, like the Titanic's little sister, and it's absolutely packed. Gobs of frat boys are already making a good time for themselves by mixing batches of funky drinks, gutting out watermelons for punch bowls, and poking umbrellas into coconuts-turned-drinking-mugs. One of the Delta Pi guys takes our tickets to check us in and explains where our rooms are. Meanwhile, another one comes over with an armful of Hawaiian leis. He tosses a big fat purple one around my neck. "Aloha," he says. "Wanna get *leid?*"

"No, thanks," I mutter. I give him a slight smile, but apparently that isn't good enough. The guy is completely beaming at me.

"Stacey . . ." Amber says, elbowing me, most likely to urge me to play along and flirt back. But I'm here on business. "Don't mind her," Amber says to him after a pause. "Stacey's just a little premenstrual. Nothing that a good lei won't cure." She crowns me with a pink one, and we move down the deck as directed.

There are a bunch of girls here as well, most of them huddled up in packs, scoping everything out. I spot Casey's ex-girlfriend by the snack table. She pauses from crunching down on a stick of celery, her eyes narrowing on me the moment we make eye contact, like maybe she recognized me from that day with Clara at the Clam Stripper.

I look away, in search of Clara. There's a large open area with bolted-down lounge chairs and tables with umbrellas and a steaming hot tub off to the side.

"Do you want me to hang around for a little while and help you find her?" Amber asks.

I shake my head and give her my bag. "I'll just be a couple minutes."

"You sure?" Drea asks.

I nod.

Amber reminds me where our room is, hands my bag off to PJ, her personal bellboy, and they all head downstairs.

Meanwhile, I look back toward the dock, wondering if Clara has even gotten here yet, if maybe I should go and ask the guy who checked us in. I peer over in that direction. That's when I see him. When my insides light up like a million tiny fireflies.

Jacob.

thirty-four

Jacob doesn't even stop for a lei before heading in my direction. I wrap myself around him, feeling more than ever how connected we are, how much I truly-madly-deeply love him. I pull him closer against me, breathing into his skin, noticing how he smells like lemongrass. How I never want to fight with him again.

"What are you doing here?" I ask. "What happened?"

But instead of answering, he just looks at me, his eyes all serious, his lips slightly parted.

"What's wrong?" I ask, feeling my smile droop.

"Nothing," he says, trying to grin. "We can talk about it later." He touches the side of my face with the back of his hand, but it's almost like he's studying me, trying to read into me for some reason.

The boat horn sounds, interrupting us, indicating that we're on our way. "Wait," I yelp. "Clara . . ." I leave Jacob a moment to hurry over to the guy checking people in. I ask him to check that Clara's here, that she's on board. He runs his finger down the list and nods when he spots it. "Yup," he says. "Room thirty-one."

"Is everything okay?" Jacob asks, now at my side again.

I breathe a giant sigh of relief and hook arms with him. "Yes," I say. "For now, everything is just as it should be."

I offer to help Jacob get settled before checking in on Clara but he shakes his head, making me promise to come by his room later to talk.

"Of course I'll stop by." I squeeze his hand, noticing right away that he's still studying me again, that his jaw is locked, and his face is completely serious. "What's wrong?"

"Just be careful, okay?"

"Of course." I squeeze his hand a little harder, noticing how his palm is all clammy, how the tips of his fingers pulse into my skin.

"I worry about you is all," he says.

I kiss his cheek, lingering at his neck a moment, knowing full well that there's more to his worry, that he's not telling me everything—yet again. "I should get going," I say, finally. "Where's your room? I'll come by as soon as I can."

Jacob smiles finally, taking my hand and leading me down the stairs, down the hallway, and toward his room. I feel my face scrunch up when I notice his room number. I check it against Clara's; it seems their rooms are separated by no more than a tiny hallway bathroom.

"How did *that* happen?" I ask.

Jacob smiles a little wider. He puts his bag down so he can sandwich my hands. He kisses my palms, reminding me of his concern, telling me that he paid extra to get a room of his own, one right next to Clara's, bumping a foursome of boys to a cubbylike space shoved way in the corner.

"You're way too good," I say, planting a big and mushy kiss across his lips.

Jacob retreats into his room and I knock on Clara's door. She opens it right away. "Stacey," she perks. "So glad to see you. Is Jacob here, too?" She looks past me into the hallway.

I nod. "He's just next door." I gesture in that direction but then stop myself, wondering why she even cares.

"I had a feeling he'd come," she says, practically bubbling over now.

"Well, you're obviously feeling better," I say, remembering how sulky she seemed yesterday (post-Chad hookup) and then this morning, during my visit.

"Are you kidding? I feel *fabulous*. I mean, have you seen this place? I feel like a movie star."

"We still need to talk," I say.

"Sure." She opens the door wider, revealing three other girls. "This is Sara, Krista, and Melanie."

"Hi." I wave.

"We're roomies for the night." Clara giggles.

The three other girls, two of them sporting baby-Ts with the letters PU across the front, look less than excited over this bit of news. They all exchange looks with one another over Clara's excess enthusiasm.

"Can we go someplace?" I ask her.

"Actually," Clara says, looking back at her new friends, "we were just heading upstairs to hang out on the main deck."

"Doubt it," one of them says, her shimmery pink lips all bunched up like she just ate something sour. She cradles a towel around her neck, covering up her tan lines, gestures for her bottle-blond friends to follow along—they do—and they all head out, leaving Clara in the proverbial dust.

"So I'll see you later," Clara calls out to them.

"It's okay, Clara," I say, eager for her to come down to Earth for just five full minutes.

"What is?"

I shake my head and enter the room, closing the door behind me. "We need to stick together for the next couple days."

"Is something wrong?"

"You know there is." I take a deep breath, feeling myself get jittery from just the mere idea of having to spill it to her like this. "I know the day."

She cocks her head and unzips her bag, pulling out a hairbrush. "What day?"

"*The* day," I say. "I dreamt it. The day you're supposed to die."

Clara responds by stroking the length of her hair, moving into the mirror to fix her crooked part.

"Well?" I ask.

"Well *what*?"

"Are you even listening to me?"

Her mirrored reflection peeks up at me. "Of course I'm listening, but what can I do? I can't change your dreams."

"It's tomorrow," I say, swallowing hard, "which means we're going to be spending a lot of time together over the next couple days. As of 11:30 tonight, consider yourself surgically attached to my hip."

"11:30?" she chirps. "That sounds perfect. I mean, I *want* you to help me."

I take another deep breath, letting it out over three full beats, trying to ease the broken-glass feeling in my chest.

"Should we go find your friends?" She turns from the mirror to face me. "I mean they're here, aren't they? I'd really like to straighten things out with Drea."

I clench my teeth, loathing the fact that she's not taking all of this seriously.

"Did she and Chad get a room together?" she continues.

"Clara," I say. "Forget Drea and Chad. You could *die* tomorrow."

She looks away, back into the mirror to continue stroking her hair. "I trust you. I mean, maybe that sounds naïve, but it's just like Drea said—you're not going to let anything bad happen to me, right?"

"I'll try, but still—"

"Exactly." She smiles and turns from the mirror, wrapping her arms around me in a best-friend hug. I make an effort to hug her back, but she feels so cold that I just want to pull away.

thirty-five

Clara breaks out her make-up pouch, telling me to give her a couple more minutes of primping, after which she'll meet me up on the deck for some girls-only chit-chat with Amber and Drea. Fan-freaking-tastic.

I count to ten and make my way up there. Amber and Drea have scored themselves a couple of lounge chairs, just steps from the hot tub.

"Hey!" I call to them.

Amber makes room for me at the end of her lounger, and I plop down right away, eager to tell them about Jacob, about how he made it aboard after all.

"At least one of us has a real man." Drea sips from her gutted-coconut, umbrella-adorned drink, managing a less-than-sincere, tight-lipped smile.

"You and Chad will make up," Amber tells her. "You always do."

"Not if Little Miss Ho-Ho has anything to say about it, I'm sure."

"Speaking of the world's cheapest cookie . . ." Amber nods in Clara's direction.

She's all smiles as she makes her way toward us. "Hey, you guys!" she beams. "Isn't this boat the greatest?"

"I can barely contain myself," Amber says, a giant plastic smile stretched across her face.

"By the way," Drea tells me, ignoring Clara, "we put your bags in the room."

"If you can even call it a room," Amber interrupts. "It's more like a closet. And even worse, it's right next to Chad and PJ's room. We can't even get away from them for one miniscule night."

"Next door or not," Drea says. "I'm staying as far away from Chad on this cruise as I can."

"I'm sorry," Clara says. "I didn't mean to start problems between you guys. I honestly didn't know you two were that close."

"Um, yes, you did," Drea says, her eyes widening to show annoyance.

"Honestly," Clara asserts. "I mean, he hardly ever mentions you."

"Don't you have some other relationship-wrecking to do?" Drea asks. "I think I saw a happy couple over by the punch bowl."

"Joke all you want," Clara says. "But just remember, even *you* said you guys were fighting. Plus, you have to admit, Chad doesn't seem like the commitment type, at least not to me."

"Maybe that's because he'd never commit to someone like *you*."

"Ouch," Amber whispers.

I open my mouth to interrupt just as the loud and bellowing blow horn sounds, followed by one of the frat guys announcing that dinner is being served.

"Saved by the blow," Amber says.

I nod in agreement.

Apparently they've got a barbecue going on the other side of the boat. The smell of burning charcoal mixed with sweet and sticky marinades is thick in the air. People begin moving in that direction, leaving the hot tub completely unoccupied.

"Opportunity's knocking, ladies. I say we dive in." Amber peels off her shorts and top, revealing a tie-dye pink bathing suit that matches her rubber sandals. She slips those off as well, pushes the button that turns on the jets, and then sinks down into what looks like foaming bubbly bliss. "Sheer heaven," she says, leaning back against one of the jets.

"That looks way too good to pass up." Drea follows Amber's lead, pulling off her cotton tank dress, glancing in Clara's direction as she settles her itsy-bitsy, teenie-weenie bikini-suited body into the water. "Stacey, you *have* to get in here."

I look at Clara. "Do you want to come in, too?"

"Sure." She nods. Though she doesn't look so sure. She nibbles at her lip, tightening up the slit on her sarong, watching Amber and Drea the whole time, obviously sensing the fact that she's not welcome.

I pull off my T-shirt and jean shorts and slip my plum-purple tankini-suited self into the foamy water.

"Better than chocolate, eh?" Drea says, smiling for the first time today.

"Better than a lot of things," Amber says, arching her eyebrows up and down.

"Are you coming in?" I ask Clara.

She sits down on the edge of the tub instead. "Maybe not. I have this thing about swimming in public pools."

"It's a *hot tub*," Drea says, correcting her. "And there's probably enough chlorine in here to kill off even the strongest of parasites."

"What's that supposed to mean?" Clara asks, wiping a splash that's landed right below her eye.

"Nothing," Drea says, eyeing her manicure.

I do my best to block them out, concentrating on the soothing quality of the jets. But I couldn't feel more tense. A part of me agrees with Drea; she has every right to be steaming, quite literally, over the predicament. But I also know I can't judge. I mean, Clara's right; it was less than two years ago that I practically did this exact same thing—that I kissed Chad, knowing full well that Drea was still in love with him. This fact, pig-piled on all of Jacob's secrets and the added stress of having to save Clara, makes me want to slip under the silky water and spiral down the drain.

"Maybe I've pruned enough," Amber says, perhaps feeling a bit of the tension as well. "Anybody for a weenie?"

"None for me, thanks," Drea says. "But I'm sure Clara will take one."

"Or two." Amber giggles.

I give them a stern look, but it's too late. Clara stands up. "I'm leaving," she announces.

"I hope it's not something we said." Drea fakes a pout.

"Don't go," I say. "They didn't mean anything."

Clara leaves anyway, wiping her eyes as she takes off down the deck.

"Thanks a lot," I say, lifting myself out of the water. "Is it so hard for you guys to be civil to her for one measly evening?"

"I tried," Drea says. "I don't know what happened."

"*That* was trying?" I grab my T-shirt and pull it on over my head.

"Stacey—wait," Amber says. She pulls herself out of the tub as well. "I'm sorry. Do you want me to go talk to her?"

"We'll both go." Drea sighs.

"Forget it," I say. If it wasn't for Jacob, I'd obviously be on my own.

thirty-six

I end up having to knock a bunch of times before Clara actually comes to the door.

"Yeah?" she asks, peeping her head out through the door crack.

"I'm sorry about Drea and Amber," I say. "They mean well, it's just—"

"Forget it." She looks over her shoulder into the room before closing the door behind her and joining me out in the hallway. "We need to keep quiet," she whispers. "Melanie got in a fight with her boyfriend. She's trying to get some rest. She's pretty upset about it."

I take a deep breath, reminding myself that I'm on duty here, that Clara's life depends on it—whether I believe she's a backstabbing ditz or not. "Well, they wanted to come down here and apologize for themselves," I say, pulling at the truth.

"Don't worry about it," she says. "I'm not mad. They have every right to be angry at me. I screwed up."

"Are you sure?"

"I'm fine. I'm just gonna stay with Melanie. She shouldn't be alone right now."

"I don't know," I say. "Maybe you should be with me."

"What happened to 11:30?" she asks. "You said so yourself—I'm not in danger until tomorrow, and tomorrow doesn't start until midnight."

I glance down at my watch. It's just after nine. "Okay, maybe we could both use a little break, but I'll be back at 11:30, not a minute later."

"Sounds perfect-o," she says, with a giggle.

I ignore her peculiar enthusiasm, reminding her that if she needs me I'll be right next door in Jacob's room. I take a couple steps down the hallway and knock on his door.

"Hey," he says. "Did you find Clara?" He peers over my shoulder to look for her.

"I'm alone." I shut the door behind me. "But as of 11:30 tonight, I'm surgically attaching her to my hip."

"Oh yeah?" he says. "And what are the chances that I could I get surgically attached to your other hip?"

"Jacob—" I laugh.

But his face is completely serious, the corners of his lips turned downward.

"What's wrong?" I ask.

"Nothing. I'd just feel better if I could be with you, if I could help you."

"Why do I feel like there's something you're not telling me?"

He shakes his head and looks away, avoiding eye contact.

"What is it, Jacob?" I press.

"Just let me help you," he says, staring down at his fingers.

"You know something."

"Yeah," he says, finally looking back at me. "I do. I know that if I were in trouble, you'd want to be there to help me, both emotionally *and* physically."

"Wait, who says I'm in trouble?"

"Nobody." He sighs. "But why risk it by working alone?"

"Who says I'm alone?" I ask him. "Of course I want your help. We're a team."

"Good," he says, with another sigh.

I lean against his chest, allowing him to cozy me up in his embrace. It feels so good to be held like this, by him—sometimes I forget how much.

"Have I mentioned yet how lucky I am?" I ask.

"Nope." He smiles.

"Well, I am," I say, nuzzling a bit deeper into his T-shirt. He smells scrumptious—like sea salt and lemongrass. "So, now what?" I whisper.

Instead of answering, he just kisses me—a warm, delicious kiss that sends goosebumps down my arms and makes my head feel all dizzy. Jacob takes my hand and ushers me inside the room. There's a eucalyptus candle sitting on his night table, the flame flickering up, the melted wax skirting out at the base. He grabs the blankets off his bed, spreading them out on the floor, picnic style. "We still have a couple hours—let's make the most of our time."

I look at him, into his slate-blue eyes, and feel my heart beat fast, my blood start to boil up. "I guess we haven't exactly been the happiest couple lately."

"It isn't your fault."

"I guess it's both our faults. I just don't want to fight anymore."

"Then let's not." He takes my hands and faces me. "At least not tonight. Let's take a break from secrets, from being jealous—"

"From being bitchy?" I add, thinking about some of the things I've said lately, how I got angry at him yesterday for *not* being jealous. "What did you have in mind?"

"I thought we might do a union spell to focus on breaking down barriers, burning away the power that secrets hold."

I nod, hoping that such a spell can work, wondering if it's a barrier that keeps me from telling Jacob how I truly feel about him. Or maybe I'm using Jacob's secrecy as an excuse to keep that barrier up. Whatever the reason for all this negative energy, it can't be healthy, so I'm more than happy to burn it away.

Jacob squeezes my hands, his cheeks turning slightly pink, like what he's feeling is emanating right through his skin. "Are you ready?" he asks, swallowing hard.

I swallow, too. And look away, hating myself for doing so. For not being able to wrap myself around him completely and whisper into his ear how much I love him—how much I head-over-heels, two-swans-forever *love* him.

"I love you," he says, doing this exact thing to me. He wraps me up like a favorite gift and whispers these three gigantic words into my ear, and all I can do is say them back inside my head, and kiss his cheek, and hope he doesn't mind the silence.

We sit down on the covers, and Jacob reaches up to pull a bottle from the night table. He shows it to me.

"Ylang-ylang oil?" I say, reading the label.

"Have you ever used it before?"

I shake my head, knowing of its sensual qualities, how it has the ability to open the senses and ease the nerves.

"Neither have I," he says. "I picked it up at the herbal shop downtown. I've been saving it for a while, but maybe now might be a good time to give it a try."

I nod, wondering what he means, what he plans to do with it. He pulls another bottle from the table—almond oil—and pours a couple tablespoons into a ceramic bowl, followed by a few droplets of the ylang-ylang. The spicy exotic scent overpowers the sweet smell of almonds and makes my head spin slightly.

Jacob dips his finger into the mixture, swirling the two liquids together until they become one pale yellow color. He faces me, his eyes almost watery.

"Are the fumes too strong?" I ask.

He shakes his head and looks away.

"Then why do you look so sad?"

"I'm not," he says, looking back at me, the wells of his eyes about to overflow. "I just want everything to be okay."

"It will be," I assure him. I take his hand, his oily fingers so soft and warm against my skin. "We're working together now. Everything will be fine."

"I know."

"Then what?"

"I guess I just want to be close to you." And with that, the tiniest tear strays from the corner of his eye.

I lean in to kiss it, to kiss him, to run my fingers down the length of his arms, hoping he knows that it's him I want to hold me always.

Jacob responds by running his oiled fingers along my neck and up my chin. "I thought we might try a little aromatic massage," he whispers. His lips are so close, his eyes zooming right into mine, making me feel all off-balance, but in a good way—a way that feels oddly stabilizing.

"That sounds good."

He pulls off his T-shirt, revealing his tanned upper body and the smooth, velvety skin, but there are scratches, too—claw marks, like from a cat, all across his chest.

"What happened?" I ask, running my fingers over them.

"A bad dream."

"Do you want to tell me about it?"

He nods. "I want to tell you everything—just not now. Tomorrow, I promise."

I nod, confident in his reply, that he will tell me everything—when he's ready. Jacob watches me watch him—his toned upper body and the ripples of muscle down his abdomen. It makes me want to crawl beneath his skin and wrap myself up in him, to lose myself in his spicy scent.

I pull off my T-shirt as well, revealing my tankini top with its crisscross straps. I tug at the hem, working it over the extra inch of snacking around my waistline, but Jacob interrupts me, as though reading my mind. He kisses me again, whispering into my ear how beautiful he thinks I am, how much I mean to him, how he'll be with me always.

He reaches into his duffel bag and pulls out a silver candle. Tall and thin, the wax almost twinkles beneath his fingertips. He sets it in a holder, rubbing more of the almond oil down the length and around the circumference to consecrate it. "As above," he whispers. "And so below."

"It's beautiful," I say, referring to the shimmering color.

"It's for secrets," he says. "To help burn away the strength they've held over us. To help us remember what's really important."

"That sounds perfect."

Jacob lights the candle and we sit and watch the flickering for several moments, reveling in the warmth of the room, the combination of soothing scents. I concentrate on the hint of eucalyptus tied with the ylang-ylang, noticing how completely at ease I feel, how unbelievably at peace.

"I'll start." I dip my fingers into the oil mixture and position myself behind him. I begin at his shoulders, working the oils into his skin, noticing how warm it feels beneath my fingertips.

"That feels amazing," he says, his voice all moist and dewy, like the room.

I kneed my fingers into his muscles, noticing where his shoulder blades meet his ribs, how the back of his neck has freckled a bit from the sun. I move myself in front of him and glide my fingertips down his chest and over his stomach, loving the way his skin feels—so slippery and smooth.

"Are you okay?" Jacob asks, probably noticing the heat I feel is visible on my face.

I nod, feeling his breath at my forehead. I look up and he kisses me—a kiss that softens, like velvet and warm honey.

He swirls his fingers into the oil and begins at my shoulders, working his way down to my hands. I close my eyes, feeling him massage tiny spirals inside my palms and down my wrists. He moves around to my back and threads his fingers around the straps of my tankini—instant jolt material. Not just my heart. My whole body.

"Still okay?" he asks.

Okay? I feel amazingly *perfect*. For the first time in my life, I want more than anything to be one with someone— to be one with *him*—completely.

I glide the straps down my arms to free up my shoulders, and then we sink down into the blankets, illuminated only by the soft glow of the silver candle.

"Are you sure?" he asks.

I nod. "I love you," I say, the words flowing out my mouth as naturally as my own breath.

With that, Jacob drapes himself over me with kisses and love.

*   *   *

The sun is so bright I can barely see. It sits alone in the sky, a perfect golden circle that reflects its rays down over the ocean. I move out onto the beach, the powdery sand warm and gritty beneath my feet, and I stare out at the ocean. The tide is coming in, bringing with it the sun's golden ripples—more beautiful than anything I've ever seen.

The ocean breeze flies through my fingertips and combs back my hair; it rustles the bamboo wind chimes, bonging somewhere in the near distance. I feel awake—more awake than I've ever known. And yet I'm asleep. I know this is a dream. A trickle of blood rolls down my cheek, like a tear. But I have no idea why I'm crying.

A few moments later, I see it—him. The man from my dream. The one carrying the bouquet of death lilies. He rolls in with the sun and waves, treading through the water to get to the beach. I squint to try and make out his face and, as he gets closer, I can see it.

It's Jacob.

He approaches me, his eyes full of tears, the bouquet of death lilies pressed against his chest—like it's his, like it's a part of him.

"No!" I yell out.

But Jacob just shakes his head and looks down.

"No," I say, wiping the blood-tears from my eyes so I can see. "Those lilies aren't for you. It's not your time."

Jacob gets about two feet away from me. I reach out to touch his face, but my fingers end up passing through him.

And then he disappears.

"No!" I scream, dropping to the ground, rocking back and forth on my knees. "You can't leave me. Not now. Not ever."

thirty-seven

I wake up alone and look at the clock. It's 11:28.

Where's Jacob?

I throw on a T-shirt and pull on one sneaker, barely even getting the back on over my heel, all the while telling myself that he's just in the bathroom or getting some air. I look around for the other shoe. There's a mound of blankets on the floor. I yank them up, revealing my other sneaker and, beside it, a folded-up piece of paper.

I grab the paper, eager for it to be a note from Jacob telling me where he went off to. I unfold it and look down at the handwritten words:

> WE NEED TO TALK ABOUT STACEY.
> MEET ME ON THE MAIN DECK AT 11:15
> TONIGHT. COME ALONE AND DON'T
> TELL ANYONE. STACEY'S LIFE
> DEPENDS ON IT.

My mind whirls with questions. What does this mean? When did Jacob get this note? Why didn't he say anything about it?

I press my fingers into the paper's grain, trying to sense something. Death—it crawls up my arms and around my neck, like a million hungry ants.

I drop the note and whip the door open, the sound of bamboo wind chimes all around me. Someone has hung several sets along the hallway, probably to promote the whole Hawaiian theme.

I bang on Clara's door.

"Yeah?" One of her roommates pokes her head out through the door crack.

"Clara," I manage, all out of breath. "Where is she? Where's Jacob?"

"Who?"

"Clara," I repeat.

"Wait—are you Tracey?"

"No . . . Stacey."

"Right," the girl nods. "She said she'd meet you on the main deck." She goes to close the door, but I wedge my foot into the door crack to keep it open.

"Excuse me?" I wipe at my nose, a dribble of blood smearing against my finger.

"Are you deaf?" The girl rolls her eyes at me. "The main deck. She said something about meeting her boyfriend."

I whirl around and run down the hallway, my mind scrambling with even more questions. What is she up to? Why didn't Jacob wake me up? Is he okay?

Why did I have that dream about him?

I bolt up the stairs, two at a time. There are voices every-where; people are still partying it up—the sounds of girls squealing, guys laughing, and bottles rolling across the wooden floor.

"Jacob," I call out, my eyes tearing up, my heart about to explode inside my chest. I follow the voices up on the deck, but I don't see him anywhere. Just groups of private par-ties—people in the hot tub and lounging on beach chairs. I move to the other side of the boat, a horrible twisting feel-ing in my gut.

I swallow hard; blood rushes down the back of my throat. Still, I keep moving forward, accidentally tripping over a cleaning bucket and barely catching myself. It's just so dark, just a few sparse lights strategically placed around the deck.

"Have you seen Jacob?" I ask some faceless guy in my path, but I don't even stop long enough for an answer.

Finally, I reach the other side of the deck. That's when I see Clara. She's standing in one of the spotlight beams, fac-ing me, but she doesn't say a word.

"Clara," I say, almost startled by her. "Where's Jacob?"

Her eyes bore right into me, almost haunted, so black against her pale white skin.

"What's going on? Where's Jacob?" I repeat.

"Taking a shower," she whispers. "You just missed him."

"What are you talking about?"

"You're a smart girl," she says, gesturing toward the blanket that's spread out on the deck. There's a picnic basket on it, as well as dinner candles, a bottle of champagne, two glasses, and a sprinkling of rose petals. "How does it feel to have someone you love taken from you?"

My jaw locks. "Nobody's taken Jacob from me."

"It didn't take much for him to stray, you know. I just told him how I caught you and Chad kissing a bunch of times on the beach and how I promised you not to say anything. I also told him how you're always complaining about how secretive he is and that you plan to break up with him as soon as the vacation ends."

"Those things aren't true," I say, noticing how both the wineglasses are completely full, as though untouched.

"*He* believed me . . . was more than happy to wipe all memory of you away. That's what the picnic was for. Of course, we never quite got around to picnicking."

I shake my head, knowing in my heart that she's lying about Jacob. I divert my eyes toward the ground, noticing a spattering of blood. I check my nose; it's dry.

The blood trails across the deck, toward the bathroom. I look up to see if Clara's noticed it too. That's when I spot the knifelike letter opener clutched in her palm. Her other hand is clutching her middle. There's a giant patch of blood there, sopped into her T-shirt. Some of it has worked its way down her waist, trickling down her thigh, and pooling at her feet.

"Oh my god, Clara, what happened?" I move toward her, almost tripping over a long metal pipe that rolls across the deck.

"I'm fine," she whispers. "Just *leave me alone.*" Her voice is weak. Her body wavers to keep a solid stance.

"What happened?" I repeat.

"I said leave me alone."

"No—let's get you some help; you're bleeding."

Instead of responding, she leans over the railing, breathing the night air in like she can't get enough, like it's helping her stay alert.

I move toward her anyway.

"Stay back," she says, snapping to attention. She whirls around to meet my gaze, her eyes wide like a cat's.

"Who did this?" I ask, just a few feet from her now.

"You did," she whispers. "You cut me. You stabbed me in the back." She sways a bit, stumbling against the railing, taking a couple steps from side to side to gain her footing.

"No," I say, taking another step toward her, keeping my eye on the letter opener in her hand. "I didn't."

"Donovan was the only boy I ever loved," she says, looking away, her eyes all teary. "You took him away from me."

"What are you talking about?"

"Maybe he didn't love me then," she whispers, "because of Drea—because he thought he was in love with her at the time. But that doesn't mean he wouldn't have fallen in love with me eventually."

I'm shaking my head, trying to make sense of what she's saying, trying to digest the fact that she even *knew* Donovan.

"Don't I look even a little bit familiar to you?" she asks.

I study her a moment, remembering how earlier Amber said she looked familiar.

"I was a sophomore last year at Hillcrest," she continues. "Donovan was kicked out the year before, when I was a freshman. Ring any bells?"

I feel my mouth drop open.

"I'm almost surprised you don't recognize me," she says. "I guess a little makeover goes a long way—either that or you and your self-absorbed friends are too preoccupied to notice anything that goes on outside your pathetic little circle."

"Clara," I say, ignoring her twisted logic, "let's get you some help. You aren't safe here." I go to peer over my shoulder, wondering where Jacob is, but notice her fingers grip tighter around the letter opener. Facing me now, she brings it up to her middle, the tip red with blood. She cradles her stomach so closely, almost as if she's holding herself in.

"Don't you get it?" she whispers. *"Nobody's* after me. Nobody's stalking me. Just like nobody was stalking Drea. Donovan loved Drea. Maybe if he didn't get locked up, if you didn't twist everything all around, he could have loved me, too. He could have seen how much I loved him."

"Clara," I say, "you don't understa—"

"No, *you* don't." She brings the letter opener up to her forearm now, grazing along her skin with the blade, as though slicing at the tiny arm hairs. "You should've heard how stupid you sounded—all that crap about me being in danger. It's just like Donovan said, you don't know how to mind your own business. I came here because I knew where you guys were vacationing. I heard you all bragging about it in the cafeteria last year—'*Aren't we so special to get a beachfront cottage*,'" she mimics. "Someone needed to teach you a lesson—you and your so-called predictions. And now I have."

"Wait," I say, hearing the metal pipe as it rolls somewhere behind me, wondering how far back it is, if I might be able to grab it. "You made this all up? You aren't getting stalked?"

She shakes her head and lets out a laugh. "I'm not even here with my parents—they think I'm at a friend's summer camp." She looks down at the scratches on her arm, the ones she said were from the doll, and runs the blade over them. It's then that it hits me—how comfortable she is with the action. How it's obvious that she's the one who cuts herself.

I glance at her sarong, the tie flapping in the breeze, imagining all the cuts she must have beneath it, remembering hearing once that people who cut themselves often pick places on their body where nobody else can see. "You cut your stomach," I say, more of a statement than a question. I take a step closer, noticing how distant her eyes look.

Clara ignores me, leaning back against the railing for support. Her feet are unsteady with the swaying of the boat—and with how weak she seems. "I hope I've made you and all of your friends' lives miserable," she whispers, "just like you've made mine and Donovan's." She goes to say something else, but the boat starts to rock a bit more, causing her to lose balance. She falls back against the railing—hard.

"Clara, be careful!" I shout.

She goes to gain better footing, but the boat rocks even harder and her body launches backward against the railing again, her feet flailing upward.

I grab her arm, yanking her forward to keep from flipping off the boat.

"Let go of me!" she shouts.

I move to steady her, placing my palm over the handle of the letter opener. I look at her, silently asking her permission to take it.

"I said, stay back!" she shouts, lunging at me with the blade. She plunges it deep into my forearm.

I hear myself wail. I go to pull the blade out. At the same moment, Clara grabs the pipe that's been rolling around the deck; it's about the length of a baseball bat. She comes at me with it, as though possessed by her own rage.

The letter opener finally free of my arm, I point it at her to protect myself.

"Clara—no!" It's Jacob. I turn to look. At the same moment, Clara strikes down on my shoulder with the pipe. The letter opener goes flying from my grip. I hear myself cry out from the sting of her blow. My whole arm is throbbing. Blood is trickling down over my fingers from the blade's puncture wound.

"Back against the railing!" She holds the pipe high, as though to strike down at my head.

I do what she says, plotting the whole time about how I can protect myself—push her back and off balance, kick her in the stomach, wait for the boat to rock and dive into her middle . . . I scan the deck for the letter opener. It's just inches from her feet.

Jacob begins walking toward us as Clara smacks down on my other shoulder with the pipe. "Stay back!" she shouts at him. "Or I'll make Stacey pay."

Jacob stops. My arms and shoulders throb with pain. I dive down for the letter opener, just as Clara stomps her heels down onto my hands. I try to pull away, but she grinds harder into my knuckles and holds me there. I lift my head, ready to bite at her ankle. Out of the corner of my eye, I see Jacob coming toward me again.

"Against the railing," she shouts at him. "Every step you take just makes it worse for your girlfriend." She plunges the pipe down into my neck, cutting off my breath, my cheek flat against the deck now. "Of course, you weren't exactly calling her your *girlfriend* a little while ago," she continues. "That's what you were calling *me*." She releases her hold on my hands to gain a better stance, and then kicks the letter opener away.

I go to push Clara back, but I can barely breathe. I feel my arms flail out, my fingers searching, reaching. I can see Clara struggling with the pipe, trying to hold me in place and keep her balance, but still, it's like there's this fire blazing inside her, feeding her adrenaline, keeping her strong.

"Let's make a deal," she breathes. "For every step your cheating boyfriend takes backward, I'll release the hold on your neck. Deal?"

I blink in agreement.

Jacob hesitates, but then I see him comply. He takes a step back and I'm able to swallow. He continues to take steps backward, toward the railing, as Clara's pipe-grip on my neck gives and I'm able to breathe. Lying on my side, I gasp a few times, keeping my eye on the letter opener, now just a few feet away. Clara follows my gaze, allowing me to sit up and push her—hard. I plunge my palms into her middle and she goes reeling. The pipe shoots from her grip. I lunge to grab the letter opener.

At the same moment, I hear it. The railing gives way and Jacob falls backward.

I stop breathing.

His scream is like a long, sour wail that cuts right through my heart. I cry out his name and scramble to my feet, running across the deck to where he fell. I look down into the ocean, half expecting to see him, but there's just blackness, the inky black water splashing up against the sides of the boat. And we're moving so fast, the boat speeding away. "No!" I cry out. "Stop!"

I go to grab a life preserver, almost tripping over the pipe that continues to roll around the deck. That's when I notice that it's actually the pin they use to keep this section of railing closed, that this is actually the gate where we boarded the boat, and somebody didn't put both pins back in.

I throw the preserver into the ocean and lean over the side of the boat. "Jacob!" I scream, over and over again, toward the water, readying myself to dive in. There's a patch of blood at the side of the boat, like maybe he hit his head.

I look back at Clara, wondering if I still need to protect myself against her attacks, but she's lying facedown in a puddle of her own blood. I approach her, noticing how her sarong has opened slightly, how there are dried cuts up and down her thighs. She's whimpering now, cradling her stomach wound. Her eyes are drooping, the fight inside her finally dead. I go to touch one of her hands, noticing how cold it feels, how her lips look blue.

I run as fast as I can to find one of the few crew members. And when I do, I can't seem to get the words out fast enough—how Jacob fell in, how the boat needs to stop and turn back.

And how Clara is minutes from death.

thirty-eight

Everything that happens next is a blur. The boat stops. The Coast Guard arrives. Rescue boats speed out. Clara is flown away in a medical helicopter.

The police come. Frat boys get arrested. Another boat ferries most of the passengers away.

And I just sit here, emotionally welded to the deck, just feet from where Jacob fell in, waiting for him to surface. I feel like if I leave this spot, he might not be able to find his way back up.

Blurs of people approach me. They want me to go to the hospital as well, I think. They want me to move away from the scene of the accident. They want me to talk to some-one, tell them everything that happened, put on a warm coat, have something cold to drink, get my arm bandaged up.

But I won't. Because that means leaving this spot, leav-ing Jacob. And I can't.

Amber and Drea are all arms and hugs around me. They're crying too, whispering that everything will be okay, that the rescue team will find him.

I hope they're right. I hope this is a horrible dream, that in a few short hours I will wake up out of this nightmarish state, even though I know it isn't.

And I know I won't.

I think I see blurs of PJ and Chad. I think they sit behind me for a while. Maybe one of them pats my back. Maybe one of them whispers that they're being forced onto the ferry. Maybe Amber tells them to go.

Maybe not.

"Stacey," some lady mouths. And then there's more mouthing, but I really don't have time to focus on all that. I have to watch the water.

I have to be alert for Jacob.

Time passes. The sun rises. Somehow my arm has been bandaged up. Somehow blankets have been placed over my shoulders. And there's a mug of something in front of me, a package of crackers as well. Amber and Drea are still here, I think. Every once in a while, one of them will wipe my forehead, hold my hand, kiss my cheek, mouth something at me.

Or maybe those are angels.

I'm busy watching the rescuers. More of them come and go, speeding back and forth in rescue boats that light up giant patches of sea. Some of them turn to look at me on their way back. They shake their heads and curse silently to themselves.

Some of them can't look at me at all.

"Stacey," a little voice says in my ear. "Time to go."

I shake my head, swearing that I'll never leave, that Jacob and I will never be apart.

But they take me anyway—hands and arms and fingers, pulling at me, making me go, taking me away, mouthing things at me despite my pleas to stay and wait for Jacob. "He'll find me!" I shout, so loud inside my head; I'm not sure if they can hear it, too. "I need to be here for him."

I fight all of it, kicking and screaming and weighing myself down by dragging my feet along the deck. Until I can't fight anymore. Until I feel dead inside.

Until my body gives out and my life falls to pieces.

epilogue

Fundraiser Frat Cruise Turned Booze-fest Bust Leaves One Teen Critically Injured, Another Missing

SANDYHAVEN—One teen is missing, another was rushed to Morley General Hospital during what was supposed to be a charity event sponsored by Pinewood University's Delta Pi fraternity.

The young man missing is Jacob LeBlanc, 18, of Vail, Colorado. According to authorities, LeBlanc had been trying to resolve a scuffle between two female passengers when the boat deck's railing gave way and LeBlanc fell overboard at around 12:05 AM Friday morning.

According to Officer James Riley of the Sandyhaven Police, a pin holding the railing together was either taken out or became loose, allowing the barrier to become unhinged.

The Coast Guard arrived shortly after LeBlanc's fall. No body has been recovered.

The teen flown to Morley General and involved in the incident is said to be in stable condition. Earlier in the evening, the 15-year-old female, whose name has not been released, stabbed herself in the stomach, according to

Riley, and had to receive an emergency blood transfusion.

Riley says authorities have been unable to determine if the stabbing was accidental or a suicide attempt.

The exact cause of the incident is unknown. One source says the 15-year-old may have been pretending to be the victim of a stalking as a way to get close to LeBlanc and his girl-friend, Stacey Brown, 18, who was also involved in the scuffle. Brown was treated for minor injuries at the scene.

The source says the girl had been leaving gifts and mysterious notes for herself, claiming that they were from an anonymous stalker. Parents of the 15-year-old declined to comment, but a friend of the family says the teen's parents thought she had been vacationing at a friend's summer rental.

Brown also refused to comment.

A criminal investigation is underway, and police say the search for LeBlanc will continue for another 72 hours.

"It just isn't right," Riley said. "He [LeBlanc] and his girlfriend were set to start college in just a couple weeks. Now his parents are planning his funeral."

Transcript from therapy session
with Dr. Atwood

[Begin tape]

Dr. Atwood: How are you feeling today?

SB: Numb.

Dr. Atwood: Understandable. Do you want to talk about it?

SB: Not really.

Dr. Atwood: I want you to know that what you're feeling is completely normal. It's good to give yourself time to grieve. It's healthy. We need that.

[Long pause]

Dr. Atwood: Do you want to talk about what happened after the accident?

SB: Not really.

Dr. Atwood: What would you like to talk about?

SB: Nothing.

Dr. Atwood: Have you tried drafting that letter we talked about?

SB: No.

Dr. Atwood: I really think it might help you, Stacey.

SB: [shrugging]

Dr. Atwood: I was thinking . . . it might also be helpful to write a letter to Clara.

SB: No!

Dr. Atwood: I know the idea of it might seem overwhelming right now, but it might give you an outlet for some of your anger. Even if you don't send it, it'll give you a place to explore your feelings toward her, toward her actions.

SB: I hate her.

Dr. Atwood: Tell me why.

SB: You know why.

Dr. Atwood: It's good for you to get it out. Tell me, why do you dislike Clara so much?

SB: Because she's responsible.

Dr. Atwood: For what?

SB: For what happened.

Dr. Atwood: What specifically?

SB: All of it.

Dr. Atwood: What do you think her plan was?

SB: To cause problems.

Dr. Atwood: Problems for whom?

SB: Everybody.

Dr. Atwood: Including you and Jacob?

SB: [nodding]

Dr. Atwood: Why do you think Clara would want to cause problems between you and Jacob?

SB: Because of Donovan.

Dr. Atwood: The boy who was sent to the juvenile detention center?

SB: [nodding again]

Dr. Atwood: She blames you for that?

ME: [more nodding]

Dr. Atwood: She must have been very angry.

SB: I don't want to talk about it anymore.

Entries from Jacob's journal

Monday, August 23 rd
Moon: last quarter

    I had another nightmare. It was even more intense than the last one. I dreamt that I was choking. My lungs were filling up with water and I couldn't breathe. I woke up in a cold sweat with a horrible stabbing feeling in my chest. I fear I'm going to drown.

    I want to tell Stacey about it, but it seems she's having nightmares about some girl who's renting down here as well. She seems really stressed about it. I figure if I just stay out of the ocean, away from water, I should be okay. Except Stacey keeps asking me to go for a swim. I feel like a jerk keeping secrets from her, but I know it's for the best. If she had any idea that I was going to drown, that my life was at stake, she'd drop everything. That's just the way she is. I don't want to add that stress to her right now.

    Tonight, after everybody goes to sleep, I'm going to the beach to do a prophecy spell with saltwater, sunflower seeds, and dried thyme. I hope it tells me what I need to know. Am I really going to drown? What's going to cause it? Is it purely accidental or is someone else behind it?

    And then I need to stop it from happening.

Tuesday, August 24th

It's getting harder to keep my nightmares a
secret from Stacey. I know she suspects something's up. I also know it's causing a rift between
us. Maybe I should tell her. But every time I
want to, it's like it's never the right time. She's
beyond stressed, like I've never seen her
before. Who knows? Maybe part of her stress is
because of me. Maybe she can sense something
about me and what I'm dreaming. But I know
if she suspected anything bad, she'd come
forward about it. Wouldn't she?

Of course she would. I think the nightmares
must be playing with my mind. They're getting
worse. Last night I thought I died right in my
sleep. I woke up, clutching my skin, making sure
I was still alive. There were scratches across
my chest. I think I must have dreamt I was
struggling to find my way above the surface of
the water and scratched myself in the process.

I woke Chad up as well. He asked me what
was wrong and I told him I had a dream about
falling. I think he believed me because he didn't
ask more, but it doesn't matter. All that matters
is that I figure everything out.

Wednesday, August 25th

Stacey wants me to go on this frat-party cruise. But obviously I can't. I can't go out in the water. I'm almost surprised she hasn't recognized that yet. She insists on going because Clara is going. I don't know about Clara. There's something I don't like about her—though it doesn't seem like anybody likes her.

I bought Stacey's ticket for the cruise, but I know it doesn't help. I know she wants my support. I don't know what to do anymore. I hate all these secrets. But I'd hate it even more if Stacey ditched helping Clara because of me. If something bad happened to Clara, Stacey would feel beyond guilty. I know she would.

Tonight, after everyone's asleep, I'm going to sneak out and try some crystal magic out on the beach. It's easier to get away at night, plus I have the moon's energy. I feel like it's really obvious when I take off during the day, like today. I know Stacey was hurt when I just left like that at the Clam Stripper. It's just sometimes I need to do a spell when the sun is at its peak. I know it bothers Stacey. I know she notices. I hate keeping stuff from her.

Thursday, August 26th

I had a nightmare this afternoon and it totally freaked me out. Instead of dreaming about my own death, I dreamt about Stacey's, that she was going to die tomorrow. In the dream, she was drowning instead of me. I was there, trying to help her out of the water. I think I may have even jumped in, but it's like I couldn't reach her, like she was just inches from my fingertips, slipping farther and farther away by the moment. I woke up in a panic, breathing hard, practically panting, I think.

When I woke up, there was a note stuck to the window from the outside. It had my name written across it. I'm not sure what it means.

If anything happened to Stacey I think I'd die as well. I need to be with her today, every day, no matter what.

If anything happens to me, I want Stacey to have this journal.

Anonymous note to Jacob
(stuck inside his journal)

JACOB,

IF YOU DON'T COME ON THE CRUISE,
I PROMISE YOU, YOUR BELOVED
STACEY WILL DIE.

More from session with Dr. Atwood

Dr. Atwood: You mentioned once before that you sensed that Clara was in danger.

SB: [nodding]

Dr. Atwood: Did you tell her about your premonitions?

SB: [nodding again]

Dr. Atwood: So let me get this straight—you were having premonitions about Clara; she thought they were fake, but, all along, she was truly in trouble.

SB: Yes.

Dr. Atwood: Quite a coincidence, don't you think?

SB: I don't believe in coincidence.

Dr. Atwood: What do you believe?

SB: [shrugging]

Dr. Atwood: You want to know what I believe?

SB: [more shrugging]

Dr. Atwood: I believe that maybe, unknowingly, you gave Clara the whole stalker idea. I think that maybe when she saw how concerned you were about her, she knew it would be a good way to play it up, pretend to be the victim of a stalking. It would be a good way to get close to you and cause problems.

SB: [shrugging again]

Dr. Atwood: I also believe you might be a little confused about things—about what you say you predicted, about what you believe you sensed. But that's understandable; you've been through a lot.

SB: It doesn't matter what you think.

[Long pause]

Dr. Atwood: A psychologist I spoke to at Morley seems to think that Clara was a "cutter." Do you know what that is?

SB: [more nodding]

Dr. Atwood: The psychologist believes Clara's stomach wound might have been accidental—that she'd been trying to cut herself and pressed too far. From what I understand, the wound was pretty extensive. If you hadn't been there, she probably wouldn't be around right now. How do you feel about that?

SB: [shrugging again]

Dr. Atwood: Did you know a photographer who was renting a cottage near yours?

SB: Where did you hear about him?

Dr. Atwood: I heard on the news that he was being questioned—something about taking pictures of young women on the beach.

SB: [more nodding]

Dr. Atwood: Clara also took pictures—of herself, correct?

SB: [nodding] Using the timer on her Polaroid.

Dr. Atwood: Interesting. I wonder if she wanted you to think that the photographer was the stalker.

SB: It doesn't matter.

Dr. Atwood: Why not?

SB: [sighing] All that matters now is finding Jacob.

Dr. Atwood: And you believe he'll be found?

SB: It's fine if you don't. It doesn't matter what anybody else thinks.

Dr. Atwood: It's been four weeks, Stacey.

SB: Without a body, they can't declare someone dead at sea for seven years.

Dr. Atwood: So you plan to wait seven years?

Letter to the Admissions Department
at Beacon University

September 1, 2004

Casey Devon
Director of Undergraduate Admissions
Beacon University
223 Tremont Street
Boston, MA 02116

Dear Mr. Devon:

My daughter, Stacey Brown, is currently enrolled to start as a freshman at your university in a couple weeks. Unfortunately, I'm going to have to ask that you defer her admission until the spring 2005 semester.

Stacey is dealing with the trauma of losing her boyfriend. I'm sure you've heard that Jacob LeBlanc has been missing for several days now. I know he's enrolled to attend your university as well.

As I'm sure you can imagine, Stacey has not been herself lately. She, Jacob, and Stacey's friend, Amber Foley, were all so excited when they all got into Beacon, but unfortunately, her admission will have to wait a few more months.

Thank you in advance for your patience and understanding. Please let me know if you have any questions.

Sincerely,

Maureen Brown

More from therapy session

Dr. Atwood: Tell me, Stacey, do you normally feel you can sense danger the way you did with Clara?

SB: Sometimes I dream about danger. I was dreaming about her death.

Dr. Atwood: Hmmm . . . Interesting.

SB: Why?

Dr. Atwood: Because you told me last time that Jacob was dreaming about death as well—about your death, his own death . . . and yet, according to you, nobody is dead.

SB: Just me.

Dr. Atwood: You feel like you're dead, Stacey?

SB: Inside, I do.

[End tape]

Letter to Jacob

Dear Jacob,

My therapist told me that I should write to you. She said it would be an opportunity to say goodbye. But I'll never say that. I miss you, Jacob. I can't even tell you how much.

I've decided to stay here, at the cottage. Amber is staying with me, deferring her admission as well. I just can't leave you here. I mean, what if you came back and I'd already left? I'll never leave you, Jacob.

I got your journal. Your mother gave it to me. She and your dad flew in from Colorado almost immediately. When your mother was cleaning your stuff from the cottage, she found it lying out on your bed. She saw the dedication—to Stacey, forever, with love—and gave it to me. I still haven't been able to go into your room.

I read your entries from cover to cover. I wish you would have told me about your nightmares. I wish you would have asked me for help.

I wish a lot of things.

I go over and over in my mind everything that happened that night, everything I could have done differently. If only I had identified that stressful feeling I kept getting in my heart, nearly cutting off my breath. If only I had taken another route up to the main deck when I saw Clara's note—maybe we wouldn't have missed each other. If only I recognized the railing pin earlier—maybe I could have warned you.

If only.

I haven't told anyone this, but sometimes I can still feel you. It's like you're somewhere out there, trying to get to me, sending me vibes that you're still alive.

Sometimes when I'm asleep, I have to force myself to wake up because I can feel you inside me. I can feel my nerves pulsing beneath my skin, my blood boiling up, and my breath quickening. I roll over in bed, feeling your fingers kneading down my back, your breath on my neck, and your lips at my shoulder.

Just like that night.

I've been sitting out on the beach a lot, looking out at the ocean as it rolls up to meet me, hoping to see you walking up the beach, greeting me with a kiss, telling me how much you love me.

And me telling you how much I love you back.

Sometimes I see the rescue team go out. They tell me it's just a matter of time before they find it—your body. That's what they're calling you now. But maybe I don't want them to find you. Maybe somewhere deep inside me I believe you aren't in this sea—that by some miracle of miracles you got away, that you didn't drown, that you got saved by some fishermen or floated away on some magical piece of driftwood.

I light a thick white candle, just like we did that night last November when we silently declared our love for one another. I place the candle beside me in the sand. The flame represents you. I know that if my grandmother were here she'd tell me that as long as I keep your memory alive, your spirit will be with me always.

I know in my heart that's true.

Always and forever,

Stacey

THE END

www.FluxNow.com

Where young adult is a point of view, not a reading level.

Hosted by Flux Acquisitions Editor Andrew Karre, our blog at Fluxnow.com is a place where we share the book experience with the new literati: teens who are just looking for a little more respect when it comes to what they read. You won't find condescension or over simplification here. Visit us online for author interviews, commentaries, gossip, contests, and more.

You have the ear of the publisher—tell us what you think.

Ordering Information

Order Online:
• Visit our website www.fluxnow.com, select your books, and order them on our secure server.

Order by Phone:
• Call toll-free within the U.S. and Canada at
  1-877-639-9753
• We accept VISA, MasterCard, and American Express

Order by Mail:
Send the full price of your order (MN residents add 6.5% sales tax) in U.S. funds, plus postage & handling to:

> Flux
> 2143 Wooddale Drive
> Woodbury, MN 55125-2989

Postage & Handling:
Standard (U.S., Mexico, & Canada). If your order is:
  $24.99 and under, add $3.00
  $25.00 and over, FREE STANDARD SHIPPING

AK, HI, PR: $15.00 for one book plus $1.00 for each additional book.

International Orders (airmail only):
  $16.00 for one book plus $3.00 for each additional book

Orders are processed within 2 business days. Please allow for normal shipping time. Postage and handling rates subject to change.

Nightmares. Dark Dreams. Premonitions of Death.

Welcome to Stacey's world...

Blue Is for Nightmares
0-7387-0391-5 • $9.95

"I Know Your Secret..."

Stacey's having nightmares again. Not just any nightmares—these are too real to ignore. The last time she ignored them, a little girl died. This time they're about Drea, her best friend who's become the target of one seriously psycho stalker. Everyone thinks it's just a twisted game . . . until another girl at school is brutally murdered.

White Is for Magic
0-7387-0443-1 • $9.95

"I'm Watching You..."

One year later, it's happening again. Seventeen-year-old Stacey Brown is having nightmares. What's worse is that she's not the only one having weird dreams. A new guy claims that he's been having nightly premonitions of Stacey's death for months. Will their dark dreams come true?